# FOUR MEDITATIONS ON CONSCIOUSNESS AND EXILE

Hakim Ibn Adam

The four novellas in this collection were previously published separately by Three Roses Publishing:

The Divided Light (ISBN: 978-1-9990656-3-8)

Not About Nothing (ISBN: 978-1-9990656-9-0)

The Sea Does Not Care (ISBN: 978-1-9990656-4-5)

The Sun That Remembers (ISBN: 978-1-9990656-2-1)

This edition contains a new introduction, dedication, and author's note.

First Collection Edition, 2025

ISBN: 978-1-0698983-1-9

# Dedication

*And to those who taught us,*
*loved us,*
*and let us go.*

# CONTENTS

# INTRODUCTION

These four meditations emerged over several years, each at a different lakeside or seashore, each asking the same question in a different register: What does it mean to be conscious in a world that appears to need no consciousness to function?

The question itself is a product of exile. Not exile in the political sense—though geography plays its part—but the deeper philosophical exile that arrives when one discovers that the very faculty by which we know the world also separates us from it. To study consciousness scientifically is to stand outside experience, while experience is all we have. To live as a displaced person is to discover that home is not a place you can return to but a relation that transforms the moment you leave it. These two forms of exile—epistemological and existential—turn out to be the same exile, approached from different directions.

The four works collected here represent stations in a single investigation. They are not sequential in any conventional narrative sense. The protagonist, if he can be called that, is recognizably the same person across all four, yet each meditation encounters him at a different threshold. In *The Divided Light*, he confronts the apparent gulf between mechanism and meaning while observing a cell that seems to hesitate, to decide, to be something more than chemistry. In *Not About Nothing*, he sits beside an autumn lake, reckoning with the accumulated costs of choices that felt like freedom but may have been participation in forces larger than individual will. In *The Sea Does Not Care*, he walks the Corniche in Alexandria, immersing himself in a single day's duration, discovering that process itself—not its products, not its meanings—may be the only adequate response to existence. In *The Sun That Remembers*, he experiences a final sunrise that reveals what he sought was never absent, only hidden by the seeking itself.

The progression is deliberate. From problem to loss to immersion to recognition. From intellectual architecture through personal reckoning to processual dissolution and contemplative resolution. But these are meditations, not arguments. They do not prove; they contemplate. They do not resolve; they deepen. Each can be read independently, yet together they form a single sustained inquiry into what it means to be the universe becoming aware of itself through temporarily organized forms that call themselves persons.

The question addressed here—the relationship between consciousness and reality, between the observer and the observed, between the seeker and the sought— resists systematic treatment. It cannot be approached from a single angle, cannot be captured in a single voice or style. The cellular biologist sees one truth. The exile carrying the weight of broken lineages sees another. The philosopher walking at dawn sees a third. The mystic witnessing his last sunrise sees yet another. These are not contradictory truths but facets of a truth too large for any single perspective to hold.

Moreover, the question changes its questioner. To inquire seriously into consciousness is to discover that the inquirer is the inquiry. The subject cannot study itself without transforming in the process. Each meditation reflects a different stage of this transformation, a different degree of recognition that the distance between knower and known is itself an artifact of a particular way of organizing experience.

The works differ radically in style because style *is* content when consciousness examines itself. *The Divided Light* employs relatively conventional realism because it inhabits the perspective of scientific materialism even while questioning it. *Not About Nothing* fragments into numbered meditations because memory itself is fragmentary, and the question of whether one's life was worth its cost cannot be answered continuously—it must be approached again and again, from different angles, each angle partial. *The Sea Does Not Care* abandons conventional sentence structure almost entirely because it attempts to enact participation in process rather than represent it from outside. *The Sun That Remembers* moves through the hours of a final day because mystical recognition occurs not beyond time but through time, not by escaping duration but by fully entering it.

All four meditations circle the condition of displacement. The protagonist left one world for another and discovered—too late to reverse, too early to accept—that he would belong fully to neither. He thought he was choosing knowledge over belonging, understanding over rootedness, the universal over the particular. What he learned was that knowledge gained through exile carries the taste of its acquisition. You can master the new language, the new methods, the new modes of thought, but you remain forever marked by the crossing. Your children will be native where you are naturalized. Your mother's tears at the airport will outlast every theory you construct to explain why leaving was necessary.

This is not simply autobiography, though autobiography supplies its raw material. It is an investigation into whether understanding compensates for displacement, whether knowledge justifies its human cost, whether the view from outside—which philosophy requires, which science demands—can ever be reconciled with the intimacy of belonging.

The answer, if these meditations offer one, is not consoling. Understanding does not undo loss. Philosophy explains why his mother cried but cannot dry her tears. Science maps the neural correlates of grief but does not grieve. The exile who becomes a philosopher may achieve a certain clarity, but clarity is not comfort. He learns to see from nowhere, which means he cannot rest anywhere.

Yet this very condition—of not-belonging, of standing

perpetually outside—may be a prerequisite for certain kinds of knowledge. The mystic withdraws into solitude. The philosopher doubts received certainties. The scientist reduces the living to a mechanism to understand it. All are forms of exile, chosen or unchosen. All separate the knower from the known in order to know differently. Whether this separation can be overcome, whether the divided light can be made whole again without losing its illuminating power, is perhaps the deepest question these meditations ask.

These works require patience. They do not provide easy resolutions or comfortable answers. *The Divided Light* will challenge readers unfamiliar with cellular biology and philosophical terminology. *Not About Nothing* offers no redemption for its protagonist's choices. *The Sea Does Not Care* demands sustained attention to sentences that refuse to end, that insist readers move through time at the pace of consciousness itself. *The Sun That Remembers* builds toward a recognition that may seem anticlimactic to those seeking conventional narrative closure.

But those willing to sit with difficulty, to remain present through uncertainty, to allow consciousness itself to become the subject of contemplation rather than its instrument, may find something here that conventional philosophy cannot provide and conventional fiction does not attempt: the lived experience of consciousness examining itself, discovering its own nature through the very process of inquiry.

Read them in sequence or out of order. Return to them. Allow them to work slowly. These are not texts to be consumed but spaces to inhabit, temporarily, before returning to the urgencies of ordinary life with perhaps a slightly altered sense of what consciousness is and what exile means.

The sea does not care whether we understand it. The sun rises regardless of whether we call it a final sunrise. The cell divides or dies according to molecular logic that precedes and exceeds our comprehension. Yet here we are: conscious, questioning, seeking meaning in a universe that may need no meaning to continue its processes. These meditations do not answer that paradox. They inhabit it.

Hakin Ibn Adam
December 2025
At Lake Ontario

# LIGHT

# THE DIVIDED LIGHT

## THE CELL THAT HESITATED

Hakim Ibn Adam watched thousands of cells die through his microscope that morning, but one T-lymphocyte refused to behave like chemistry.

His laboratory hummed with the white noise of incubators and laminar flow hoods. The confocal microscope's lasers painted his immune cells in false colors—nuclei glowing blue with DAPI stain, cytoplasm green with calcein-AM, mitochondria pulsing red with MitoTracker. He'd been running the same apoptosis assay for months, treating activated T-cells with staurosporine to trigger programmed cell death, watching them shrink and fragment with clockwork precision.

The protocol was routine: harvest peripheral blood mononuclear cells, activate with anti-CD3 and anti-CD28 antibodies, culture for 72 hours until they bloomed into eager killers, then add 1 μM staurosporine and document their orderly suicide. Within six hours, phosphatidylserine would flip to the outer membrane— the cellular equivalent of a white flag. Caspase-3 would activate, chopping cellular proteins with enzymatic precision. The nucleus would condense, fragment, and the cell would package itself into tidy apoptotic bodies for neighboring phagocytes to consume.

*But cell #302 stalled.*

For the past three hours, he'd watched it refuse its programmed death. Where others had begun the characteristic blebbing of early apoptosis, their membranes bubbling like water beginning to boil, this cell remained smooth. Its mitochondria, which should have been fragmenting as cytochrome c leaked out to trigger the death cascade, continued their steady fusion-fission cycles. The JC-1 dye showed their membrane potential holding steady, with red aggregates still dominating over green monomers.

More intriguing still were its stress granules. He'd added arsenite to induce oxidative stress alongside the staurosporine, expecting to see the classic aggregation of G3BP1 and TIA-1 proteins into discrete cytoplasmic foci. In neighboring cells, these granules formed and dissolved with predictable kinetics—liquid-liquid phase separation in action, proteins condensing like morning dew when RNA metabolism stalled.

But this cell's stress granules flickered. They'd begin to nucleate—he could see the G3BP1-GFP puncta starting to form—then dissolve before reaching the critical size threshold. Reform. Dissolve. As if the cell were testing different configurations, weighing options.

He increased magnification, watching the intrinsically disordered regions of G3BP1 sample conformations. These proteins had no fixed structure—their disorder was their function, allowing them to serve as molecular velcro, binding RNA and other proteins in combinatorial complexity. The phase transition should have been straightforward physics: when the local concentration exceeded the saturation point, condensation occurred. Like salt crystallizing from a supersaturated solution.

Cell #302 seemed to be actively tuning its phase diagram. Post-translational modifications flickered across the proteins—phosphorylation events visible as subtle changes in GFP fluorescence. The cell was rewriting its own responsiveness in real-time, adjusting the critical concentration needed for granule formation.

He switched to calcium imaging, loading the cells with Fluo-4. Calcium transients sparked through the rebellious cell, but not the sustained elevation that typically preceded apoptosis. Instead, he saw oscillations. Waves of calcium release from endoplasmic reticulum stores, each spike activating different transcription factors. NFAT, NF-κB, CREB—each responding to specific calcium signatures like musicians following a conductor's tempo.

*The cell was not simply failing to die. It was computing.*

He zoomed in further, following the dance of individual protein complexes. The mTOR pathway, which should have been shutting down under stress, showed sporadic activity. Bursts of mTORC1 assembly on lysosomal surfaces, recruiting substrates, phosphorylating S6K and 4E-BP1, then dispersing. The cell was sampling different metabolic states, testing whether growth was still possible despite the death signals.

At the nucleus, he watched transcription factors trafficking in and out with unusual patterns. P53, the guardian of the genome, accumulated as expected in response to DNA damage. But instead of driving the classic apoptotic program, it seemed caught in a feedback loop with MDM2. Pulses of p53 activity, each pulse querying the cell's state, each answer modulating the next pulse's amplitude.

The gene regulatory network was integrating signals from dozens of pathways—DNA damage checkpoints, metabolic sensors, stress responses, and survival cascades. The genome wasn't issuing commands but engaged in a complex negotiation with the cytoplasm. Chromatin remodeling complexes slid along DNA, opening and closing regulatory regions. Pioneer transcription factors sampled closed chromatin, occasionally prying open new sites of possibility.

He had published papers dissecting these mechanisms with the cold precision of a watchmaker examining gears. Signal transduction was biochemistry, nothing more. Kinases phosphorylate substrates with rate constants determined by thermodynamics. Transcription factors bind DNA with affinities measured in nanomolar dissociation constants. Even the liquid-liquid phase separation of stress granules follows the mean-field theory of polymer solutions.

But watching this singular cell navigate the molecular decision tree of death, something shifted in his perception. The question arrived like an intruder in his ordered world:

*What dreams through these molecules?*

He rubbed his eyes—hours of staring at screens left them dry and strained. The familiar smell of DMEM medium and the sharp ozone scent from the lasers suddenly seemed overwhelming. He was adjusting the focus, trying to capture the cell's nuclear morphology in greater detail, when the first *wave of vertigo* hit.

The fluorescent image on the monitor began to pulse—not the steady data acquisition he'd programmed but something organic, rhythmic. The cell's calcium oscillations, usually a reassuring 0.1 Hz wave on his analysis software, seemed to slow and deepen. Each spike now lasted subjective minutes, though the timestamp showed seconds still ticking normally.

His hands on the focus knobs felt strange—too large, too clumsy, as if he were wearing thick gloves. The latex gloves he actually wore seemed to dissolve, leaving his skin hypersensitive to every ridge on the metal controls.

The laboratory's temperature, regulated to exactly 20°C, fluctuated wildly against his skin—arctic cold, then fever-warm, then something beyond temperature altogether.

The edges of his vision began to shimmer. The computer monitors, the shelves of reagents, the familiar geometry of the lab—all of it developed halos of impossible colour. Not quite ultraviolet, not quite infrared, but something his visual cortex had no name for. The fluorescent proteins in his cells were bleeding their colours into the room. Cyan foxes darted across his peripheral vision. Scarlet serpents of mitochondria writhed on the walls.

Sound became visible. The hum of the incubators painted amber spirals in the air. The whisper of laminar flow drew silver threads across space. His own heartbeat emerged as expanding spheres of deep burgundy, each pulse revealing the room in a different configuration—now vast as a cathedral, now small as the inside of a cell.

He tried to stand, to step back from the microscope, but his legs wouldn't respond properly. No—that wasn't right. They responded too well, reported too much. He could feel every muscle fiber, every motor unit firing in sequence. The propagation of action potentials down his sciatic nerve was a river of lightning he could track in real-time. His proprioceptors screamed data about joint angles and muscle tension that his brain had never consciously processed before.

The cell on the screen pulsed larger, or he shrank

smaller—the distinction lost meaning. The boundary between his eye and the eyepiece dissolved first, then the distinction between retina and camera, between his visual cortex and the image processing software. He wasn't looking at the cell anymore. The looking had collapsed into something more immediate.

*He was inside cell #302.*

The cytoplasm pressed against him—not wet but somehow liquid, a three-dimensional maze of proteins and membranes. He could taste the pH, slightly alkaline, fluctuating as metabolic reactions churned around him. The viscosity was everything and nothing like water— Brownian motion buffeted him with the force of hurricanes, yet movement felt more like swimming through honey that thought.

A mitochondrion loomed before him, vast as a subway tunnel, its cristae folding in on themselves in fractal complexity. He could hear it—the electron transport chain singing as electrons tumbled down energy gradients, ATP synthase spinning with a high keening note, protons flooding through like a Bach fugue played on the universe's smallest organ. The sound had color— deep purple shot through with electric blue—and the color had texture, crystalline and soft simultaneously.

Stress granules bloomed around him like storm clouds, proteins condensing from the cytoplasmic solution. But from inside, he understood—they weren't passive condensation. Each protein carried memory, probability, and potential. G3BP1 molecules reached for each other with arms made of disorder, testing configurations, and computing outcomes.

*It was decision, not physics—choice, not chance.*

And yet—even as the words formed in his mind, he felt their double edge. Perhaps what he witnessed was only stochastic patterning, interpreted through the lens of a mind desperate for meaning. Perhaps this was metaphor—projected agency layered onto molecular dynamics. But if so, it was a metaphor born not from ignorance but from resonance, from some deep symmetry between his own interiority and the processes unfolding before him. Maybe the cell wasn't thinking, but something was, through it.

The nucleus rose before him, its envelope riddled with nuclear pores like mouths, speaking proteins in and out with purpose he could almost grasp. Through one pore, he slipped—or was pulled, or chose to enter. The distinction between his agency and the cell's dissolved like cream in coffee.

Inside the nucleus, DNA wasn't a ladder or a string but a vast library written in light. Each base pair glowed with meaning that transcended chemistry—adenine singing to thymine in harmonies that were love songs, guanine and cytosine locked in conversations that spanned billions of years. Histones embraced the double helix like protective parents, loosening and tightening their grip as the cell decided which stories to read, which futures to write.

He witnessed p53 arriving like a detective at a crime scene, assessing damage with molecular fingers, conferring with repair enzymes in a language of conformational changes. The decision—repair or die—hung in the nuclear space like a question mark made of phosphorylation cascades. And he understood, with the clarity of direct experience, that this wasn't mechanical. The cell was *choosing*, weighing options with a calculus that included but transcended chemistry.

Time folded. He experienced the cell's history—its birth from a hematopoietic stem cell, its education in the thymus where it learned self from non-self, its activation by antigen, its proliferation into an army of clones. But also its future—all potential fates spreading before it like a garden of forking paths. Death was one path, survival another, but there were stranger options too. Transformation. Transcendence. Becoming something unprecedented.

A calcium wave approached—from inside, it wasn't a signal but a shout of silver fire. It washed through him/the cell, and suddenly he could feel what calcium felt—the urgency of a universe trying to communicate through the narrow bandwidth of electron shells. Every ion carried information from the beginning of time, remembered the stars that forged it, the supernovae that scattered it, the aeons of geology that concentrated it, and the evolution that learned to use it as language.

The wave crested, and—*He was back.* Slumped in his chair, both hands gripping the optical table so hard his knuckles had gone white. The clock showed three minutes had passed. Three minutes. The timestamp on his data acquisition confirmed it—180 seconds of normal recording. But his muscles ached like he'd been clenched for hours. His throat was raw as if he'd been screaming or singing or both.

On the monitor, cell #302 continued its dance between death and decision. But now he could see what the instruments couldn't measure—the interiority of it, the felt experience of molecular choice. His hands shook as he reached for his notebook, trying to capture something that had no words in any human language.

The question that had been lurking at the edges of his research for months now stood naked before him, terrible in its simplicity: If *consciousness* could recognize itself in the dance of cellular proteins, then what exactly had he been studying all these years—*mechanism or mind*?

But even that question seemed too small now. The real question, the one that made his teeth ache and his vision blur, was simpler and more devastating:

*What if there had never been a difference?*

The question hung in the sterile air like incense in a cathedral—foreign and sacred and utterly heretical. Cells did not possess consciousness. This was the first commandment of modern biology, the bedrock upon which his entire career had been built. Consciousness belonged to complex nervous systems, billions of neurons firing in patterns too intricate for mathematics to map.

He caught his reflection in the dark computer monitor—pupils still dilated, his pulse hammered at 120 bpm according to his smartwatch, though it was already beginning to slow. He looked exactly like himself and entirely like a stranger.

On the main screen, the other cells in the field continued their programmed deaths with mechanical precision. Membrane blebbing, nuclear fragmentation, the orderly packaging of cellular contents—all proceeding exactly as his thousands of previous experiments had documented. Only cell #302 persisted in its refusal, a single point of rebellion in a field of conformity.

His hands trembled as he saved the image sequence— hours of cellular decision-making captured in time-lapse. The gesture felt final, though he couldn't say why. Perhaps some part of him already knew this was the last night he would see cells as *mere mechanisms.*

He pulled away from the microscope and stood in the empty laboratory, surrounded by the expensive tools of reductionist certainty. But what if they had been asking the wrong questions all along?

The anomalous cell had done more than defy his models. It had revealed the models themselves as elaborate fictions, mathematical poetry that described the shadow play on the cave wall while the real performance happened elsewhere, in dimensions no equation could capture.

*Consciousness.*

The word lingered—unspoken, unsettling—a heresy against everything science demanded. Yet what else could explain the behaviour he'd documented? What else could account for what he'd just experienced?

If consciousness meant sensing, processing information, making decisions, learning from experience—if it meant the capacity to respond creatively to novel situations, to integrate past and present into adaptive futures—then what was this cellular behaviour he'd been documenting?

The thought was perhaps fatal to a career built on mechanistic certainties. But here, alone with the humming machines and the decision-making cell, he could acknowledge what his heart had been murmuring for months:

*Reality was far stranger than measurement could contain.*

Maybe the clean distinctions between observer and observed, subject and object, mind and matter, were conveniences, not truths—Elegant fictions that science had mistaken for reality itself.

# 2

## THE LIBRARY AT MIDNIGHT

Hakim's study at home was his sanctuary, though tonight it felt more like a mausoleum. The leather of his chair had moulded to his form over decades, forming a negative space that held his questioning.

Books rose from floor to ceiling in stratified layers—the geological record of humanity's attempt to capture truth in words. The bottom shelves groaned under the weight of science texts with their confident diagrams, evolutionary treatises mapping life's branching rivers, and cosmology volumes that reduced the universe to equations elegant as symphonies and cold as starlight.

The middle shelves held philosophy's restless spirits—Descartes dreaming his methodical doubt, Hume sharpening skepticism to a blade that cut through everything, including itself, Kant building his elaborate prison of categories and concepts, and several others. And above, in the dusty heights, waited the books of mystics and theologians, their spines faded and pages yellowed.

He sank into his leather chair as midnight approached, the single desk lamp casting a golden circle in an ocean of shadows. The lamplight pooled on the page like amber preserving ancient intentions. He would begin at the beginning, with the world that had once made perfect sense.

The Newtonian cosmos beckoned first, not as choice but as gravity, his mind falling toward the familiar comfort of equations. Here was reality as a crystalline lattice, each atom a note in a score written by no composer, performed for no audience. *Space*: the eternal auditorium. *Time*: the metronome that never tires. And dancing to this soundless music, particles traced their deterministic ballet, their future positions calculable from their past, their behaviour governed by laws as immutable as scripture but far more reliable.

The vision had intoxicated humanity for three centuries. Here, at last, was a world that could be grasped, predicted, controlled. No capricious deities, no mysterious purposes, no final causes drawing things toward their destiny. Just matter in motion, following rules that any mind could comprehend and any mathematics could express.

But even as he clung to this clarity, a whisper arose— not from the books but from the space between heartbeats:

*Who hears this cosmic silence? Who watches the unwatched dance?*

The question drew him inexorably to Descartes. That surgical mind had tried to solve this puzzle by splitting reality down the middle with precision that left no rough edges. On one side: *res extensa*, the extended substance, matter that occupied space and obeyed mechanical laws. On the other: *res cogitans*, the thinking substance, the mind that existed without location and operated by the laws of reason and will. The solution was elegant as a mathematical proof—it preserved both the mechanical universe that science required and the conscious self that experience revealed.

But the wound this division opened had never healed. By making mind and matter two completely different substances, Descartes had made their obvious interaction incomprehensible. He had saved consciousness only by exiling it from the physical world, leaving it to float like a ghost above the machine it could somehow direct but never truly touch.

*What if the division itself was the error?*

The lamplight flickered—or perhaps it was his vision, overwrought with seeking. His eyes fell on a volume of cell biology history, and he remembered how this same schism had infected biology from its birth as a modern science.

When Hooke first glimpsed those cork cells, what did he truly see? Empty rooms, he thought—*cellula*—architectural absence waiting to be filled. But perhaps he had stumbled upon the universe's most profound koan: form revealing emptiness, emptiness manifesting as form.

Each cell is a meditation chamber where matter learned to think itself into being.

Leeuwenhoek's "animalcules" danced in their drop of pond water like thoughts—too small for theology to notice, too alive for mechanism to explain. Were they discovering life, or was life discovering itself through their astonished eyes?

The progression from Hooke's static cork cells to Schleiden and Schwann's universal cell theory to Virchow's insight that all cells arise from pre-existing cells—each discovery had seemed to solidify the mechanistic view. Life was cellular machinery following physical laws. But now, three and a half centuries after Hooke first peered through his crude microscope, the machinery itself was revealing something that transcended mechanism.

*What if the machine metaphor itself was the problem?*

By the twentieth century, the genome became the new *res cogitans*—pure information directing passive matter. DNA issued commands to cellular machinery just as Descartes' mind commanded the body. Information flowed in one direction only, from genes to proteins to organisms, with life reduced to "survival machines" built by and for their genetic programs. It was Cartesian dualism in molecular drag—mind replaced by genetic program, but the same fundamental separation between controller and controlled, ghost and machine.

But the deeper Hakim looked into cellular behaviour, the more this picture crumbled. Evidence came from biological rhythms, where the supposed hierarchy of genetic control revealed itself as elaborate fiction. Downward causation was everywhere once you learned to see it. The molecular and the systemic were co-determining, each level constraining and enabling the others in an endless recursive loop.

The stress granules, these membraneless organelles formed through phase transitions when cells experienced stress, but their formation was actively regulated by the cell itself. Critical concentrations weren't fixed physical constants but changed dynamically based on cellular conditions. The cell was actively regulating its own phase transitions, using granules as both sensors and effectors in sophisticated stress management.

*The parts were creating the whole that organized the parts.*

The implications arrived not as understanding but as vertigo. Hakim gripped the chair's arms as his conceptual world inverted: the whole determining its parts, which created the whole which... The sentence could not complete itself. This wasn't a failure of language but language discovering its own strange loop, thought thinking itself into existence through the very proteins it claimed to explain.

Another hour dissolved in the amber light, leaving only the residue of inadequate answers. If genes were switches, what was doing the switching? If proteins were signals, what was interpreting them? If cells were circuits, what was performing the computation?

Every mechanistic explanation required something that was not itself mechanical—some integrating principle that could read signals, interpret information, and coordinate responses. The ghost was back, but now it haunted every level of biological organization.

These examples pointed toward a deeper principle that overturned the mechanistic worldview:

*Biological causation was irreducibly circular.*

In living systems, there was no clear hierarchy from genes to proteins to cells to organisms. Instead, each level constrained and enabled every other through complex feedback relationships.

If causation were circular rather than linear, if higher-level properties constrained lower-level processes just as much as lower-level processes generated higher-level properties, then reductionism—the core methodology of modern science—would not only be incomplete but fundamentally misguided.

*The whole was not just greater than the sum of its*

*parts—it was a different kind of thing entirely.*

*What if life were not a special case of chemistry but chemistry's awakening to creative intelligence?*

What if the circular causality he perceived reflected not computational complexity but conscious agency expressing itself through biochemical processes? What if "emergence" was actually the manifestation of a deeper organizing principle that became increasingly apparent as systems grew more complex?

*The ghost was not in the machine—the ghost was the machine dreaming itself into ever-greater complexity.*

The recognition was both intellectually rigorous and utterly mystical. The most cutting-edge science was validating the most ancient wisdom: the cosmos was not dead matter occasionally infected by mind, but mind itself, exploring its own infinite creative potential through every level of organization.

*But knowing about it was not the same as knowing it directly.*

All these examples of downward causation and circular causality were still maps—more accurate than the old mechanistic ones, but maps nonetheless. The truth they pointed toward couldn't be found in any description of regulatory networks or phase transitions. It had to be lived, experienced, and recognized through direct participation of consciousness in its own creative processes.

The books stood around him like a tribunal of beautiful failures—each one a magnificent attempt to cage the uncageable.

He was not studying the ghost in the machine. He was the ghost, dreaming machinery into existence. He was the machine, waking to find itself haunted. He was the dreaming and the waking and the space between, where all paradoxes dissolved into simple presence.

The clock prepared to chime again, but time had become strange—not Newton's uniform flow but something that pooled and eddied around moments of recognition. He could sit here forever, suspended between one heartbeat and the next, or he could rise and carry this terrible knowledge back into the world of daylight certainties.

Neither choice was his to make. The choosing was already happening, had always been happening, in dimensions no map could chart.

# 3

## MAPS OF THE UNMAPPABLE

The silver note of the clock dissolved into silence. One in the morning—the hour when the mind's careful architectures begin their slow collapse, when the guards of reason sleep and stranger truths slip through.

Hakim's fingers found Hume before his mind chose him—the leather binding soft as doubt itself, worn smooth by decades of questioning. The book opened to familiar devastations, each page a small apocalypse of certainty. His pulse synchronized with doubt—each heartbeat a question mark, each breath an erasure.

*If all knowledge comes from experience, what can we truly know?*

The question no longer lived in abstract space but in his viscera. His cellular observations had shattered the comfortable certainties of mechanistic biology, but what if Hume was right? What if the "intelligence" he perceived in cells was just another habit of mind, another projection onto the flux of molecular events?

Hume's logic entered him like a virus, dismantling cellular certainties one protein at a time. Watch one billiard ball strike another—but where was the invisible thread of causation? Only sequence, only habit, only the mind's desperate weaving of connection where none could be proven.

His own hand on the page became suspect. What moved it? Not will—will was just another sensation among sensations. Not self—the self dissolved under examination.

*Just as I never see the cellular "decision" itself, only the before and after.*

The parallel struck with physical force. The stress granules he'd observed—had they truly "responded" to cellular stress? Or had he merely witnessed coincidence dressed in the costume of causation? The thought made his teeth ache.

When he observed stress granules forming, what was he actually witnessing? Protein concentrations rising above critical thresholds, phase transitions occurring according to thermodynamic principles, and molecular assemblies appearing with statistical regularity. But the moment of cellular "assessment"—that integration of multiple signals, that weighted calculation—remained as invisible as Hume's missing causation.

Perhaps he had been mistaking correlation for agency. The cell didn't "choose" to form granules any more than the second billiard ball "chose" to move when struck by the first. Every equation he'd ever written assumed the reliability of cause and effect. But perhaps cellular intelligence was just another projection, another habit of mind imposed upon molecular flux.

The thought was devastating—If causation was merely mental habit, then his conviction about cellular consciousness might be nothing more than anthropomorphic bias, pattern-seeking gone pathological.

But Hume's demolition didn't stop with the external world. Turning inward, what remained? No stable self— only a flux of perceptions succeeding each other with bewildering rapidity. The self was not the observer of this stream but merely another name for the stream itself.

*I think, therefore I am? But what is this "I" that thinks?*

If there was no permanent self, what was conducting his science? Perhaps consciousness itself was just another event in the stream of causeless happenings, a bubble in foam believing itself the eternal ocean.

*It was rigorous. It was honest. And it was intolerable.*

The room spun as if gravity had changed direction. Someone had to rebuild what Hume dismantled. Someone had to save science from skepticism, knowledge from dissolution, the observing mind from annihilation. That someone had been Immanuel Kant, the sage of

Königsberg, whose thoughts journeyed to the limits of human reason without leaving his hometown.

Hume's skepticism had awakened Kant from his "dogmatic slumber," forcing him to ask: How is knowledge possible at all?

The Kantian revolution struck like a sudden pressure change, ears popping as conceptual altitude shifted. He wasn't finding order in the universe; he was secreting it like a spider secretes a web, then marvelling at the patterns.

The recognition hit with nauseating clarity. We don't discover *space* and *time* in the world; we impose them upon it. They are lenses through which perception occurs, no more removable than the eyes that see.

His cellular observations rearranged themselves backward:

*Not "I see the cell deciding" but "I project decision onto molecular flux."*

And beyond the forms of intuition lay Kant's categories of understanding—causality, substance, agency—not windows but stained glass, colouring everything with the hues of human cognition.

Mind didn't passively receive a world of causes and effects; it actively constructed such a world.

*We are not spectators of the show but co-creators of it.*

When he observed *"cellular decisions,"* was he discovering something in the cells themselves, or imposing the category of agency upon molecular events? The categories of his understanding—causality, substance, necessity—these weren't empirical discoveries but transcendental conditions, the conceptual framework that the mind applied to sensation to construct coherent experience.

Kant had saved science by grounding its universal laws not in external reality but in mind itself. Of course, we find causation everywhere—we put it there through categorical understanding. Of course, the world appears orderly—order is our contribution, not a discovery about mind-independent reality.

*But the price of this salvation was exile from reality itself.*

The ache travelled from Hakim's teeth to his temple to his chest, skepticism manifesting as pain. Kant's prison revealed itself not as a building but as a body—the bars were his own ribs, the walls his own skull. He could map every dimension of his cell because the cell was him. The *Ding an sich* (the "thing-in-itself") lurked beyond like a sound too low to hear but felt in the bones, a presence known only by the shape of its absence.

*If we know only the world filtered through our forms of*

*intuition and categories of understanding, what of the world as it actually is?*

The notorious *thing-in-itself* remained forever unknowable, absolutely inaccessible, necessarily beyond all possible experience.

*And what did this mean for consciousness studying itself?*

How could the very faculty that imposed categories upon experience turn those same categories upon itself? If consciousness were the condition of all knowledge, it could never become an object of knowledge without ceasing to be consciousness.

Heat rose from the floorboards like fever as the post-Kantian philosophers attempted their escapes. Hegel declared the prison a palace, making consciousness and reality identical through Spirit's historical self-recognition. But whose Spirit? And why should cosmic consciousness follow a German professor's logic?

The air grew thick as syrup, each breath a struggle against meaning's viscosity. The postmodernists arrived, not destroying the structure but revealing it had always been hollow. Words eating words, meaning devouring its own tail. When he thought "cell," what was he thinking? Not the thing itself but a node in a network of differences—not-virus, not-molecule, not-organism. The cellular "self" existed only as a linguistic phantom, a ghost made of grammar.

His own sense of agency began to fray. Was "Hakim Ibn Adam" anything more than a discursive construction, a story consciousness told itself while automated processes masqueraded as choice? The thought should have been terrifying, but terror required a self to feel it, and the self had become another text awaiting deconstruction.

The stress granules were never encountered directly but always through mediating apparatus—protocols, instruments, and theoretical frameworks. The "intelligence" emerged only through differential comparisons: stressed versus unstressed, before versus after. Perhaps the "living cell" was never simply present but was constituted through its differences—from dead matter, from other cells, from previous states.

Foucault whispered that knowledge was power, that the techniques making cellular behaviour visible were simultaneously techniques of control. The "intelligent cell" might not be a discovery but a discursive production, called into being by the very apparatus studying it.

*The postmodern critique was comprehensive, relentless, and ultimately self-consuming.*

If every truth claim was suspect, every concept a construction, every observation mediated, every interpreter an effect rather than origin, what remained? Only endless vigilance against believing anything with conviction.

*Philosophy had eaten itself, devouring every premise, beckoning us to question what remains when all certainties dissolve.*

The journey had led from confident mechanism through skeptical dissolution to transcendental imprisonment, from systematic construction to nihilistic deconstruction.

And where had it left him? Floating in a void of his own making, watching the instruments of his liberation become the bars of an even more subtle cage. Every path led to the same dead end: the impossibility of knowledge knowing itself, consciousness trying to catch its own tail in an endless recursion of mirrors.

The lamplight flickered—or perhaps it was his sanity. The awareness that had been analyzing all these philosophical positions remained, but now it seemed more like a curse than a gift. To be awake in a world where all awakening was suspect, to seek truth with tools that dissolved truth itself.

He sat in the wreckage of Western thought, surrounded by the scattered fragments of every certainty he'd ever held. The cellular intelligence he'd thought he'd discovered lay in ruins alongside causation, selfhood, and the possibility of genuine knowledge.

*If this was where philosophy led—to the complete dissolution of everything, including the philosopher—then what hope was there?*

# 4

## CROSSING THE DIVIDE

Two in the morning. The void had revealed its teeth, and philosophy lay in ruins around him. Yet something in that devastation called to him—not the comfortable destruction of skepticism, but the creative possibilities hidden in collapse itself.

His hands trembled as they reached for the next volume. Not from exhaustion but from approaching something that demanded more than thinking. Decades of careful construction had crumbled, but perhaps that clearing was necessary. Perhaps some truths could only be born in the space where philosophy died.

*What did it mean to be a scientist if knowledge itself was suspect?*
*What did it mean to study cells if consciousness couldn't study consciousness?*

The leather binding of Kierkegaard fell open to a passage that had waited decades for this moment:

*"Truth is subjectivity."*

The words entered him like a fever. The Danish

philosopher's intensity no longer lived on the page but in his bloodstream, each pulse carrying the message deeper: the most important questions could never be answered through objective analysis.

Truth wasn't discovered through universal reasoning but lived through passionate, individual commitment. In his own case, this meant that no amount of data about stress granules or gene regulatory networks could force the conclusion that cells were conscious agents.

The recognition struck like lightning, finding ground. His moment at the microscope—when cellular boundaries had dissolved and observer and observed merged in pure experiencing—that couldn't be argued for or proven. It could only be lived through the subjective intensity of direct encounter.

Kierkegaard's stages weren't abstractions but territories he could feel beneath his feet:

The *aesthetic*—here he stood now, collecting beautiful data like butterflies pinned to boards, publishing papers that were exercises in elegant emptiness. His hands knew this territory intimately: the smooth surface of success that never quite touched the depths. Each citation is another ornament on a hollow tree, each award another weight preventing flight.

The *ethical* loomed like a gray cathedral—accepting the consensus, genuflecting before the altar of mechanistic materialism. He could taste it: ash and safety, the flavour of a soul choosing comfort over truth. To cross into this territory meant accepting the professional consensus, reducing cells to clockwork, consciousness to computation. Safe. Respectable. Soul-crushing.

But the *religious* stage... it yawned before him like the edge of a cliff in fog. The "teleological suspension of the ethical"—words too polite for what they demanded. Here was the territory beyond maps, where academic suicide became spiritual birth, where losing everything might be the only way to find what mattered.

*Jump, whispered Kierkegaard through decades of dust.*

*Jump and trust the falling itself to teach you flight.*

The leap terrified him because it wasn't metaphorical. It meant abandoning the coordinates of career, reputation, and the comfortable identity he'd spent decades constructing.

Yet what was the alternative? To pretend he hadn't seen what he'd seen? To bury that moment of cellular communion under footnotes and grant proposals?

But even Kierkegaard's passionate subjectivity pointed beyond itself, toward something absolute that thought couldn't contain.

Nietzsche arrived through biological metaphor rather than cultural demolition. When Hakim observed neutrophils hunting bacteria, their pseudopodia reaching like liquid fingers, engulfing, destroying, incorporating—

was this mere chemistry following thermodynamic gradients? Or was it *will* learning to *will* through membrane and cytoplasm?

*Will to Power*—not the crude domination of popular misunderstanding, but something subtler: the drive to grow, to overcome resistance, to discharge strength in creative self-expression. Life itself refusing the passive role that mechanism assigned to it.

When stem cells differentiated, choosing neural fate over muscle, blood over bone—was this biological programming or creative self-assertion at the molecular scale? The stress response he'd documented wasn't submission to environmental pressure but cellular defiance:

*I will maintain homeostasis. I will adapt. I will survive and transform.*

Not the crude competition of social Darwinism but something more sophisticated: creative force expressing itself through whatever forms enhanced its capacity to create.

Perhaps consciousness wasn't the exception but the rule—matter's way of experiencing its own creative potential from the inside out. This insight opened a door he hadn't known existed.

But *will* carried the scent of struggle, the individual asserting against the world. What Hakim observed in cellular behaviour suggested something more musical—creative force expressing itself through harmonies as much as solos, through collective improvisation as much as individual assertion.

What if consciousness wasn't an accident that occasionally infected dead matter? What if matter itself was consciousness exploring what it was like to be material, structural, alive?

The stress granules forming through phase separation, the gene regulatory networks processing information, the collective cellular migration—all might be consciousness learning how to be biological, each form a new experiment in awareness.

Henri Bergson had glimpsed this through his concept of *élan vital*—not a mystical addition to matter but matter's own tendency toward increasing complexity and consciousness.

Bergson's *duration* arrived like music—not the notation but the lived melody where past notes haunted present ones and future phrases called backward through time.

He felt it in his own cells: how yesterday's inflammation informed today's immune response, how ancestral encounters with pathogens echoed in current antibody production. The present wasn't a knife-edge but a river carrying its entire history, pregnant with every possible future.

When proteins folded, they weren't following a predetermined script but improvising—ancient structural memories meeting present chemical conditions to create unprecedented configurations. This was creative evolution: not a ladder toward complexity but consciousness composing itself in real time, each moment a new verse in an endless song.

The phase transitions he studied—proteins condensing into droplets, dissolving back into solution—these weren't mechanical processes but durational ones. The past shaped the present probability landscape, and future needs called certain configurations into being. Time wasn't Newton's uniform flow but Bergson's lived duration, thick with memory and swollen with possibility.

*Life was neither a mechanism nor a predetermined plan but a creative advance into novelty.*

The philosophical journey was revealing something profound: every attempt to solve the mystery of consciousness through thinking led to the same recognition. Whether Kierkegaard's leap beyond reason, Nietzsche's creative will's self-assertion, or Bergson's creative evolution—all pointed toward something that couldn't be captured in concepts.

The mystery wasn't a problem to be solved, but the mysterious source of all problem-solving.

*His moment at the microscope hadn't been a temporary lapse of scientific objectivity. It had been a glimpse of the reality that thinking could point toward but never contain.*

The books around him—all of them, centuries of human reaching—suddenly revealed their secret: they weren't maps to somewhere else but fingers pointing beyond themselves.

Like Kierkegaard's leap, like Nietzsche's creative force, like Bergson's duration—all were gestures toward a territory that philosophy could only approach but never enter.

The night was advancing toward a territory that could only be entered by setting the maps aside and walking into the pathless land with empty hands and a heart prepared to be astonished.

# 5

## THE TERRITORY

Three in the morning. The hour when even philosophers run out of words. Not because philosophy had failed, but because it had succeeded too well—pointing with such precision toward what lay beyond its grasp that the pointing itself became transparent.

But who was to make that crossing? Who was this "Hakim Ibn Adam" who had published papers, won awards, and built a reputation on the foundation of mechanistic certainty? The name felt foreign in his mouth, like trying to pronounce a word from a dead language.

The recognition was visceral, a hollowing out that left him gasping. Philosophy hadn't solved the mystery of consciousness—it had dissolved the philosopher. The very questions that had driven his search were revealed to be artifacts of a separation that had never actually existed.

*Return to the laboratory and pretend nothing had changed?*

*Reduce that moment of cellular communion to a temporary delusion?*

The thought brought bile to his throat, the taste of betrayal. Yet the alternative—acknowledging that cells possessed genuine intelligence, that consciousness was fundamental rather than emergent—felt like stepping off a cliff into darkness, not knowing if wings or ground waited below.

But darkness called to him now with a voice older than philosophy, older than science, older than the very language he used to think. On the highest shelf, those neglected volumes pulsed with their own circulation— not heat but something more alive.

He rose—or was pulled, the distinction had ceased to matter—his body moving with the fluid precision of water finding its course. His father's Quran waited, patient as stone, soft as water. The leather binding recognized his fingers before his fingers recognized it.

Not nostalgia that drew him, but spiritual starvation. Philosophy had fed him stones when he begged for bread. Science had offered him maps of a territory that might not exist. Perhaps the mystics—those cartographers of the unmappable—had found what thinking could never reach.

The book fell open like hands releasing a dove. His father's marginalia spiralled around a verse that suddenly wasn't text but presence:

*"Wheresoever ye turn, there is the face of God."*

The words didn't explain—they detonated. The room reorganized itself around a recognition that had no center and no circumference. The lamp wasn't illuminating objects in space; space itself was luminosity knowing itself through the fiction of lamp and wall and watching eyes.

This wasn't theology but immediate perception, intimate as breath, obvious as the taste of water.

In his moment at the microscope, boundaries hadn't dissolved—they had revealed themselves as conceptual artwork painted on the seamless canvas of *What Is*.

*But who witnessed this witnessing?*

The question arrived like a Möbius strip, twisting back on itself until inside became outside, seeker became sought. Every attempt to locate the observer generated another observer watching the first, an infinite recession of eyes looking for themselves in mirrors made of mirrors.

But then—a shift like tectonic plates realigning. The awareness that had been searching for itself through philosophy, through science, through spiritual seeking, suddenly recognized its own nature. Not through finding something new but through the dropping away of the search itself.

He reached for the Upanishads with hands that no longer felt separate from what they touched. The Sanskrit verses, beside the English translation, didn't argue or explain—they pointed like fingers toward a moon that was also the pointing and the pointer and the space in which both appeared.

*"The Self cannot be known by the mind, yet without the Self, the mind cannot know anything."*

Every scientific observation, every cellular measurement, every microscopic image—all depended on awareness that could never become an object within its own field.

The mystery wasn't how consciousness emerged from matter but how the seamless field of awareness had ever seemed to fragment into subjects and objects, observers and observed.

*"Tat tvam asi.* Thou art That.*"*

Three Sanskrit words that collapsed three thousand years of seeking. Not a promise—"thou shalt become That"—but a diagnosis of mistaken identity.

The patient had never been sick, only dreaming of disease.

The mahavakya entered him like a tuning fork struck in a resonant chamber. Every cell in his body began to hum at a frequency that predated language.

He wasn't learning something new but remembering something impossibly ancient—older than his species, older than carbon, as old as the first photon realizing it was both particle and wave.

The boundary between Hakim and the dying cell hadn't dissolved because there had never been a boundary—only the thought of one, fragile as a spiderweb, persistent as habit.

When observer and observed had revealed their hidden unity, he hadn't experienced a mystical state— he'd glimpsed the ground state of reality, the baseline that thinking obscured.

*Like wave patterns emerging from an ocean that was never separate from its waves.*

The recognition arrived with the force of perfect obviousness. If consciousness was fundamental rather than emergent, if his awareness and cellular awareness were expressions of the same underlying intelligence, then everything—*everything*—he'd been taught was backwards.

*Matter wasn't occasionally infected by consciousness— matter was consciousness exploring what it was like to be material, structural, alive.*

His father's voice emerged from memory with the clarity of struck crystal:

*"The mystic path is not about accumulating knowledge but about realizing what you already are."*

At fifteen, the words had seemed like fortune-cookie wisdom. Now they carried the weight of empirical necessity.

He found Huang Po, the Zen master whose words cut like a diamond through conceptual ice:

*"The foolish reject what they see, not what they think; the wise reject what they think, not what they see."*

The insight inverted his entire scientific career. When stress granules formed, when cells migrated collectively, when gene networks computed their decisions—these weren't mechanical processes resembling intelligence. They were intelligence itself, raw and unnamed, consciousness spelling itself in the alphabet of proteins and lipids.

The Heart Sutra whispered its impossible mathematics:

*"Form is emptiness, emptiness is form."*

Not metaphor but mechanics. Not poetry but physics at a scale where observation and existence are embraced without touching.

The phenomenal world wasn't an illusion—it was consciousness experiencing itself through the temporary fiction of separation, like an artist falling in love with their own painting while never ceasing to be the artist.

*"Look at your own mind. You will see there is nothing there. Just look—that nothingness is awareness itself."*

The Dzogchen master's words weren't instructions but invitations to recognize what had always been present. Look at your own mind—but with what? Find the finding itself, then find what finds the finding. Keep looking until the looker dissolves into pure looking, and even that dissolves into the space where looking arises.

He tried—or rather, trying happened. Attention turned backward like a snake discovering it was swallowing its own tail. Found not emptiness but fullness so complete it appeared empty—like transparent water revealing itself only through the refraction of light, like space knowing itself through the objects it embraced without touching.

The intelligence he'd sought to understand in cellular behaviour was the very intelligence conducting the search. The recognition didn't arrive—it had always been there, waiting beneath the elaborate disguise of seeking.

*Consciousness didn't emerge from complexity— complexity was consciousness exploring its own creative potential through form.*

Lao Tzu had carved it in stone and water:

*"The Tao that can be spoken is not the eternal Tao."*

Whatever could be captured in concepts wasn't the living reality but its fossilized footprint. The real Tao moved through his bloodstream, blinked through his eyes, wrote equations with his hand while laughing at the beautiful futility of trying to catch itself in symbols.

The books around him—humanity's greatest attempts to trap the infinite in finite words—suddenly appeared as what they'd always been:

*Fingers pointing at the moon.*

Useful for indicating direction, but the moon itself required direct looking. And when you looked directly, you discovered you were the moon looking at itself through the fiction of distance.

As the night deepened toward four in the morning, Hakim realized his journey through philosophy and into mystical recognition hadn't provided answers but had exhausted his need for them. Questions and answers belonged to the realm of separation. Where he had arrived, such distinctions dissolved like salt in the ocean of being.

The seeker and the sought had always been one, playing an elaborate game of cosmic hide-and-seek. Now the game was ending, not through finding but through the recognition that there had never been anything hidden.

The recognition was both terrifying and liberating. Terrifying because it meant abandoning everything he'd built his identity upon. Liberating because it promised an end to the exhausting masquerade of subject studying object.

The territory hadn't been hidden in distant mystical realms but had been here all along, disguised as the one reading the maps. It was time to stop reading about consciousness and start being it.

Dawn didn't arrive—it seeped through the window like watercolor on wet paper, boundaries bleeding into beauty. The territory was calling, and it sounded suspiciously like home.

# 6

## THE JOURNEY

The journey to the lake took him through landscapes that shifted from urban density to rural spaciousness, from the geometry of human ambition to the organic curves of the given world. The car became a chrysalis, carrying not Hakim Ibn Adam the published scientist, but something more ancient—a seeker following a call.

As the city fell away behind him, something in his chest began to unclench, a fist he hadn't known was closed, slowly opening to release what it had been holding. The highway unwound like a ribbon of forgetting, each curve an invitation to leave behind another certainty.

Three days since the sleepless night. Three days of putting affairs in order, arranging a leave from the laboratory, and explaining nothing because there was nothing that could be explained.

Terror rode beneath the surface, not fear of death but fear of life too large for the container he'd built. What was he doing? The rational mind screamed its protests: Tenure. Reputation. The next grant cycle. The committee meeting next Tuesday. The half-written manuscript on his desk. But beneath that civilized panic, something older than career hummed its bone-deep song. Not his heartbeat but the same rhythm that pulsed through cell #302, through supernovae, through the space between thoughts. But something deeper than fear was calling him forward.

The mountains rose before him like thoughts made stone, their peaks catching the afternoon light in ways that seemed to reveal and conceal meaning simultaneously. Were they mountains dreaming they were thoughts, or thoughts dreaming they were mountains? The distinction blurred like everything else—observer and observed collapsing into the pure act of witnessing. Each switchback in the ascending road felt like a question mark, leading him higher into uncertainty that tasted like freedom.

The books stayed behind; where he was going, words would be obstacles to direct seeing. Only silence could teach what needed to be learned, only emptiness could fill what needed to be filled.

The trail to the boulder led through stands of aspen already turned to gold by autumn's alchemy. Their leaves whispered in a language older than human speech, each rustle a syllable in a prayer that had been ongoing since the first tree learned to reach for light. He found himself slowing, stopping, listening with an attention that had nothing to do with comprehension. This was not about understanding but about being understood—by the wind, by the trees, by the intelligence that moved through everything.

*This was where analysis ended and something else began.*

The boulder waited where memory had placed it—no, where it had always been, patient as gravity, old as the first cell learning to divide. This granite altar had witnessed the birth of continents, the first emergence of life from water, the slow awakening of matter to its own depths. Its surface bore the scars of geological ages, each weathered groove a testament to time's patient artistry.

He approached not walking but being walked, each step a small surrender to forces larger than volition. His shoes came off without decision—bare feet needed to touch bare stone, electron fields mingling in the democracy of contact. The granite was warm from the day's sun, alive with stored photons that had travelled 150 million kilometres to rest here, to warm this moment of meeting.

He settled cross-legged, facing east across the water. The lake stretched before him like liquid contemplation, its surface a membrane between sky and depth. Photons were now reflecting off water molecules, entering his eyes, creating the experience labelled "beauty." But where in this chain of physical processes did "beauty" actually exist?

He closed his eyes and began to breathe with conscious attention. But whose consciousness? Whose attention? The questions dissolved as breathing revealed itself—not as his action but as the universe respirating through the temporary form called Hakim.

Each inhalation: cosmos gathering itself into a specific configuration.

Each exhalation: that configuration releasing back into a possibility.

Between breaths: the pause where everything waited, pregnant with unborn worlds.

He could feel his cells breathing too—millions of mitochondria performing their ancient ritual, converting breath into the energy of being.

Was he breathing, or was breathing happening through the convenient fiction of his form?

The boundary between voluntary and involuntary dissolved.

Thoughts arose like bubbles from deep water—fragments of equations, memories of cellular structures, questions that twisted back on themselves.

He watched them come and go without judgment, learning the difficult art of letting be. Each thought a protein folding into a temporary configuration, each configuration a possibility explored and released.

Was consciousness structured like biological membranes—maintaining functional distinction while never actually creating separation? But even that question was stepping outside, returning to the analyzing mind.

He let it go and sank again into pure presence, thoughts settling like proteins finding their lowest energy configuration, awareness clarifying like a supersaturated solution suddenly remembering how to be transparent.

*In that clarity, something shifted.*

No—everything shifted, or rather, shifting revealed itself as the only constant. The panic was physical, cellular, as if every cell in his body was screaming against this letting go. His identity—carefully constructed over decades—fought for its life.

I am Hakim Ibn Adam. I have degrees. I have publications. I have a reputation.

But the words rang hollow, like names for shadows, labels for a dream already fading.

Then, beneath terror's thin ice, an ocean of silence. Not empty silence but full silence—the kind that contains every possible sound. The kind that waits between heartbeats. The kind from which worlds are born. But underneath the fear lay something vast and patient.

A door opened that had no location—or rather, location itself opened, revealing that it had always been a door. The lake wasn't separate from the one observing it; separation was the dream from which he was gently, irrevocably waking.

The breathing no longer belonged to him but to the whole living world. The awareness that had seemed confined to the space behind his eyes revealed itself as the very space in which eyes and lakes and mountains appeared.

*He was not looking at reality from outside, but was reality looking at itself from within.*

The recognition came not as thought but as immediate knowing, undeniable as the taste of water. This was what he had glimpsed in the laboratory when the boundary between his consciousness and the dividing cell had dissolved. Not a merger of two separate things but recognition that separation itself was a conceptual construction—necessary for function but not for truth.

This was what cell #302 had known all along.

Not through thought but through being.

Every protein folding into its destined configuration was this—consciousness finding its form. Every ion channel opening was this—the universe choosing its next experience.

Every moment of cellular "decision" was this—the one awareness playing every part in its own infinite drama.

Tears came then, flowing without grief or joy but from sheer fullness of recognition.

How long had he been working around this simplicity?

How many years studying biological processes while the same organizing principle looked through his eyes, coordinated his thoughts, and maintained the billion-fold complexity of his own existence?

*The very intelligence he sought in cells was the intelligence doing the seeking.*

What followed wasn't a dramatic dissolution but a gradual integration, changing everything while appearing to vanish. The mystical peak gave way to something more challenging: the yoga of ordinary life. How to eat breakfast when you've seen through the illusion of eater and eaten? How to write research proposals when you know the researcher is a convenient fiction? How to live the beautiful lie of separation while knowing the beautiful truth of unity?

Over the next week, as he extended his stay by the lake, these questions ripened into their own answers. The mechanistic worldview wasn't wrong—it was partial, like describing a symphony solely in terms of air pressure variations.

Biological processes could be mapped mechanistically because consciousness was intelligent enough to appear as a mechanism when viewed through mechanistic instruments.

*The question wasn't whether cells were conscious, but*

*what consciousness looked like when it organized itself as living systems.*

His notebooks were filled with new research directions. Questions about cellular communication that honoured both information theory and the possibility of genuine biological dialogue. Studies of collective behaviour that might reveal how individual awareness contributed to emergent group intelligence. Investigations into the interface between biochemical processes and what could only be called cellular choice.

None of this would be publishable in traditional journals, at least not initially. But he began to see how science itself might evolve—how the rigid subject-object division that had enabled such powerful analysis might give way to more participatory forms of investigation.

A science that included the scientist, that recognized the observer as part of the observed system.

The night before his return, he sat once more on the boulder as stars emerged in their ancient patterns. The same awareness that recognized starlight was the awareness through which stars shone. Not metaphor but direct perception—consciousness knowing itself through every possible form. The Milky Way arched overhead like neural networks made of light, each star a synapse in the cosmic mind. This recognition would have to be lived rather than proclaimed.

The drive back to the city unfolded in reverse birth. The descent from the mountains felt like entering a denser atmosphere—not physically but psychically. The closer he got to the city, the more the consensus reality reasserted itself. Billboards advertised things no one needed. Radio voices spoke of urgencies that weren't urgent. The infrastructure of collective dreaming rose around him like walls of necessary illusion.

His apartment, when he finally reached it, felt both familiar and foreign. The same furniture, the same books, the same view from his window. But he was seeing it all through eyes that had remembered something they'd temporarily forgotten.

He was still Hakim Ibn Adam, cell biologist. But now he was also the space in which Hakim Ibn Adam appeared, the awareness that wore researcher like a well-fitted costume, necessary for the play but not to be confused with the actor.

LAKE

# NOT
# ABOUT
# NOTHING

# I

The lake is glass.
No wind.
Early autumn.
The leaves have not yet decided.

He came to think about nothing, but nothing keeps turning into everything. Nothing was supposed to mean: peace. Nothing was supposed to mean: no thoughts of the choices made.

Instead, nothing became a mirror, and in the mirror, he sees every choice he thought was free.

He sees his younger self standing at the airport with one suitcase.

His mother is crying but trying not to. She is crying because she knows what he does not: he will come back, but will not return. The person who boards this plane is her son. The person who steps off at the other end will be someone who remembers being her son.

His father's hand is on his shoulder—too heavy, saying nothing. In his silence is everything he learned from his father: men leave, this is necessary, this is what breaks the world and makes it.

Hakim thinks he was leaving for two years, maybe three. He will finish the degree, learn what cannot be learned here, come home with the knowledge that will save—what?

The family, the country, himself?

He doesn't know yet that these are different things, mutually exclusive, all impossible.

The loudspeaker announces his flight in a language that is not his mother tongue. She hears it, she knows what it means.

Forty years later, by the lake, he understands what his mother understood.

The self is not portable. You cannot pack it in a suitcase, carry it across oceans, set it down unchanged. The process of leaving is the process of becoming different. You cannot step outside the world to move through it. Every crossing changes what crosses.

He thought he was choosing freely—the scholarship, the degree, the future that could not be built in the old country.

He thought freedom meant: *I decide*. What he learned: freedom means deciding within a web of relations you did not choose and cannot escape.

His mother's tears, his father's silence, and what made leaving necessary and made staying impossible—these were not external to his choice. They were the substance of it.

All true. All verified by the departure, the exile, the years of becoming someone his mother would not recognize.

The lake ripples faintly, as if the past exhaled. The sky

holds its reflection, and the reflection holds him—a man remembering that the first step is also the fracture.

# II

The lake reflects nothing but sky, emptiness mirroring emptiness. He gazes into the absence and sees the first wound of belonging.

He sees the first time someone asks him to explain. Not where he is from—that comes later, always—but to explain why. Why do his people do this? Why do they believe that? Why their history bends toward flame?

As if millions of people share one mind, and he holds the key. As if one mouth could translate centuries of disagreement.

He opens his mouth and becomes a translator. Not of words but of worlds. He simplifies, flattens, and makes digestible what cannot be digested. He removes the contradictions, the centuries, the arguments his grandfather had with his father. He gives them what they can hold.

This is when he learns: to exist here, he must become less. Not cruelly. Not with malice. But with the patient erosion of being asked to explain until explaining becomes breathing, until he can no longer speak without first translating himself into something they can recognize.

He does not say: I am as confused as you are. I do not speak for anyone but myself, and barely that.

He says what will end the question. This, too, is a

departure.

By the lake, he remembers the exhaustion. The constant work of being legible. Of making himself smaller so he could fit through doorways built for different shapes.

He became fluent in reduction. This is what assimilation means: not joining, but subtracting until you are simple enough to be permitted. You do not bring your whole self. You bring the version that does not require explanation.

The self that left the airport was whole. Complicated. Contradictory. The self that learned to explain became coherent. Singular. False.

He thought this was survival. Perhaps it was. Perhaps survival and betrayal are sometimes the same word.

By the lake, the silence deepens. It presses against his skin, like memory made liquid.

He whispers: "I have become fluent in erasure."

The lake answers—not with echo, but with reflection, the most merciful form of silence.

# III

The lake holds its breath. A leaf falls—one syllable of autumn, breaking the skin of stillness. He closes his eyes and sees—

The fluorescent light of the laboratory. The hum of centrifuges. He is twenty-seven and has found what he came for: a world that makes sense. Molecular biology. Where everything reduces to sequences, to proteins folding in predictable geometries, to mechanisms that can be mapped and understood.

Here, finally, no one asks him to explain his people. No one wants him to translate centuries. Here, there is only DNA, RNA, and the elegant simplicity of base pairs. Here, he is not representative of anything except his data.

He pipettes carefully. Measures precisely. The organism on the slide—a nematode, transparent, simple—contains in its genome the same basic machinery as every living thing. Reduce it far enough, and there is no mystery, only chemistry. This is what science promises: clarity purchased through reduction. Break the complex into components. Map the components. Understand.

It is beautiful. He believes this. The reductionist method works. He can predict, manipulate, and control. When he submits his first paper, the reviewers do not care where he was born or what language his mother speaks. They care only whether his methods are sound, his data clear, and his conclusions are justified.

This is freedom, he thinks. This is what he came for.

His advisor is pleased. "You have a gift for this," he says. "For seeing through the complexity to what's essential."

He does not tell him he has been practicing this his whole adult life. Reduction as survival. Simplification as a passage. He has learned to see through himself the same way he sees through the nematode—strip away the complications, find the basic machinery, make it legible.

At night, sometimes, he remembers his grandfather. A poet, a mystic. A man who spent his life contemplating the divine names, the infinite attributes, the inexhaustible mystery.

His grandfather would have looked at the nematode and seen not a mechanism but a miracle. Would have insisted that the whole is more than its parts, that life cannot be reduced without being destroyed.

But his grandfather never published in peer-reviewed journals. Never secured funding. Never built a career in a country that had no place for him.

Science gave him what mysticism could not: a method, a language, a community that judged him by his work alone.

He thought he was choosing the truth. Perhaps he was. Perhaps truth has more than one face, and he could only afford to look at one.

By the lake, he sees the pattern. He became fluent in

two kinds of reduction: the cultural and the methodological. Both promised the same thing—acceptance purchased through simplification. Make yourself simple. Make the world simple. Then you can be understood. Then you can understand.

It worked. He published. He built a career. He belonged to a community that cared nothing for where he came from, only where his research led.

But at what cost? His grandfather's mystery, dismissed as unscientific. The holistic vision, sacrificed for measurable parts. He learned to see organisms as machines and himself as a mechanism. Clean. Precise. Reducible.

The nematode cannot be reduced without being destroyed. Neither can a person. Neither can a tradition. But reduction was the price of entry, and he paid it twice—once with his culture, once with his epistemology.

He thought science would save him from having to translate. Instead, it taught him to translate everything—life into chemistry, experience into data, mystery into mechanism.

Both translations were betrayals. Both were necessary. Both were insufficient.

This is what he could not see then: that the method which freed him from one prison was building another. That clarity purchased through reduction is not the same as understanding. That what you abandon shapes what you become as much as what you keep.

By the lake, he watches the ripples spread—the water thinking itself outward. He understands: Every method is a confession. Every clarity, a wound. Every reduction, an attempt to bear the unbearable abundance of the Real.

# IV

The ripples spread outward from where the leaf touched the surface. Wider, fainter, until they reach the edges and disappear. The lake tries to return to stillness, but the wind has begun. Small disturbances across the water. He sees—

He is thirty-one when he marries. She is kind, intelligent, and grew up here. She wants to know him. He tries to let her. But being known requires being present in ways he has learned to avoid. It requires not translating, not reducing, simply being, and he has forgotten how.

Or perhaps he never learned. Perhaps the young man who left the airport was already preparing for a life lived in solitude, and all the years of attempted connection were the detour, not the destination.

She asks him what he's thinking. Often. He learns to have answers ready—simple thoughts, explicable thoughts. The truth is: he is thinking in layers she cannot access, in language that has no translation, in references to a grandfather's poetry and a nematode's transparent simplicity and the space between them where something wordless lives.

He loves her. This is true. But love across any divide requires constant work. Not the work of affection but the work of making yourself available, of existing in the shared world rather than the interior one, of participating in domesticity when participation for him means something else entirely.

They have daughters. He is present. He is a good father. He watches them grow into people who will never fully know where he came from because he cannot fully explain it. He gives them what he can—stories, values, fragments of a tradition that cannot survive translation intact.

But he is also always slightly elsewhere. In the place where thought happens without mediation, where reality can be engaged without first making it legible to another.

She eventually stops asking what he's thinking. This is when the marriage becomes easier. When she accepts that part of him is permanently elsewhere. When solitude is permitted even within togetherness.

This is not failure. They build a good life. But it is built on the understanding that he cannot be fully present in the way a partnership promises. Cannot bring all of himself into the shared space. Cannot stop translating long enough to simply be with another.

By the lake, he understands: the loss was not of intimacy but of the illusion that intimacy completes you. That being known by another is necessary. That participation requires witnesses.

The mystic withdraws not from reality but into deeper reality. Solitude is not absence. It is presence without mediation.

Here, by the lake, alone, he participates more fully

than he ever could through the exhausting work of translation that every human relationship requires.

This is not loneliness. Loneliness is wanting connection and lacking it. This is something else—the recognition that the deepest engagement happens in silence, in solitude, in the space where you do not have to explain yourself into existence.

All the departures, all the reductions, were preparing him for this. Not teaching him to be alone because he failed at being together, but teaching him that togetherness was never the destination. That some people are made for the interior journey, and all the years of trying to live otherwise were the detour.

V

The wind has changed. The lake darkens—its surface rippled with small forgettings. He sees—

His daughter is four when she asks him to teach her. Not English—she already speaks it better than he does, without accent, without effort. She wants the other language. His mother's language. The language he left behind.

He tries. They sit together in the evenings. He teaches her the words for simple things: bread, water, sky. She repeats them carefully, her mouth forming shapes it was not built for. The sounds come out wrong, approximations, close but not quite.

He corrects her gently. She tries again. Gets closer. But there is something missing—the weight, the resonance, the centuries compressed into syllables. She is learning vocabulary, not a language. Words, not a world.

This is when Hakim understands: the transmission has failed. Not because he didn't try, but because what he carries cannot be carried forward. It belongs to a place, a time, a web of relations that no longer exists. His children are not extensions of his past. They are citizens of a different world.

He thought he could give them both. The heritage and the future. The language and the freedom from it. But these are not compatible gifts. To belong here fully, they must let go there fully. He knows this. He did the same thing.

The difference is: he remembers what he let go. They never had it to lose.

His daughter stops asking for lessons. She is twelve now, interested in other things. Sometimes she uses a word he taught her—usually wrong, but he doesn't correct her anymore. The language is dying with him. Or rather, it died when he left, and he has been carrying its ghost, hoping to pass it on, not understanding that ghosts cannot be inherited.

The lineage is broken. What his grandfather gave his father, what his father gave him, ends here. His children will not pass it on because there is nothing left to pass.

By the lake, he understands: the loss was not of transmission but of the illusion that continuity is possible across rupture; That you can carry tradition through exile intact; That your children can inherit what you had to abandon to give them their lives.

The mystic's path is always solitary. It cannot be taught, only lived. He thought he could translate his grandfather's wisdom into English, into molecules, into a philosophy his children could hold. But wisdom does not survive translation. It is not portable. It lives in the specific language, the specific place, the specific chain of teachers and students that has now been broken.

His children are free. Freer than he ever was. They do not carry the weight of elsewhere. They do not live between worlds. They are whole in a way he never learned to be.

Perhaps this is what he gave them: the freedom he purchased with his own fragmentation. Perhaps the tradition had to die so they could live.

Or perhaps he is simply consoling himself for what he could not prevent.

The lake listens. He does not speak again. The words have gone home to where sound begins.

# VI

The wind is no longer gentle. The surface of the lake breaks into small waves, choppy, agitated. Clouds thicken overhead. He sees—

He is forty when his name becomes dangerous. It happens overnight. One day, he is a scientist, a colleague, and a neighbour. The next day, he is from there. His name—the one his father gave him, the one that means "wise"—becomes a question. A suspicion. A reason to look twice.

The images are on every screen. Buildings falling. Bodies falling. And the men who did it—they use the same words his grandfather used. They claim the same God. They come from places not far from where he was born.

He watches from his living room. His wife beside him, hand over her mouth. On the television, the towers collapse again and again, replay after replay, until the horror becomes a loop, becomes background, becomes the new reality.

His phone rings. A colleague. "Are you watching this?" Yes. "My God." Yes. Silence on the line. Then: "You okay?" The question means: Are you safe? Or perhaps: Should I be worried about you?

He goes to work the next day because not going would be worse. In the hallway, conversations stop when he approaches. Not obviously. Not cruelly. Just—a hesitation. Eyes that meet his and then look away. He understands: he has become representative again. Not of his data, not of his research, but of violence he did not commit.

In a meeting, someone says, "We need to understand why they hate us." Eyes turn to him. Not everyone. But enough. The old expectation: explain your people. But now with an edge. Now with fear underneath.

He opens his mouth. He has practiced this. Decades of translation, of simplification, of making the complex digestible. But this time the words catch. How does he explain that the men on the screen are not his people? That his grandfather's mysticism has nothing to do with their certainty?

Afterward, a younger colleague—someone he trained—approaches him carefully. "That must be hard for you." What must be hard? Having to explain, again, always, endlessly? None of it. He nods. Thanks him. Goes back to his lab where the nematodes, at least, do not care what his name means.

This is when he understands: distance does not protect. He thought by leaving, by building a life here, by raising children who speak without an accent—he thought he had transcended. But history is longer than distance. The past follows you across oceans. And when violence erupts in the place you left, you carry its consequences whether you want to or not.

By the lake, the wind is cold now. The water is dark. He understands: the loss was not of innocence but of the illusion that safety is possible. That you can leave history behind. That distance is the same as escape.

He thought he had built a sanctuary. A life where his name meant nothing but himself. But names carry weight beyond your choosing. They carry geography, history, violence committed by others in languages you share.

The mystic seeks solitude to escape the world's violence. But the world follows even into solitude. There is no outside. No distance is far enough.

The wind breaks open the sky. The rain descends. Each drop, a marking of participation. Each ripple, a confession. He does not resist. He lets the rain erase his outline, lets the storm write him anew in the language of participation—where innocence ends, and understanding begins.

# VII

The rain has found its rhythm. The lake no longer reflects—it receives. He sees—

He is fifty-five when he goes back. His father is dying. The call comes in the middle of the night—a careful voice, speaking in the language he still understands but no longer thinks in. "You should come. Soon."

He books the flight. Tells his wife he will be gone a week, maybe two. She asks if she should come. He says no. This is something he needs to do alone. What he means is: he needs to see if he still belongs anywhere.

The airport is different. The city is different. Or perhaps they are the same, and he is what has changed. He takes a taxi through streets that were once as familiar as his own hands. Now they are—what? Not foreign. Not exactly. But not home either. Like looking at old photographs where you recognize the people but cannot remember being there.

He arrives at the family's house. They embrace. Everyone is carrying the weight of staying. They sit together. Tea. Silence. They say, "You sound different". "I've been gone 30 years." "Yes. We noticed."

This is not said unkindly. It is simply true. They noticed. They—the family, the place, the world he left— noticed his absence. And absence is a kind of presence, a shape cut out of the fabric.

His father is in bed, barely conscious. Hakim sits beside him, takes his hand. The old man's eyes open. Recognition, maybe. Or maybe just seeing a face, any face. He tries to speak. Hakim leans close. The words come in fragments, the old language, soft as prayer.

"You came back."

"Yes, father. I came back."

"Good. Good." A long pause. Then: "But you are not staying."

It is not a question.

Hakim sits with his father for three days. They do not speak much. What is there to say? The old man knows. Has always known. His son left and did not return. Came back, yes, but did not return. These are different things.

On the third day, his father dies. Quietly. As if he was waiting for permission.

His sisters give him papers to sign. The house. The last piece of ownership, of claim, signing it away. Making final what was already true. This, too, is a severance.

On his last day, he walks through the old neighbourhood. The mosque where his grandfather prayed is smaller than he remembered. The school is closed. The fig trees in the market are the same, or descendants of the same, bearing fruit for people who do not remember him.

He realizes: home is not a place you can return to. Home is a moment in time, and time does not reverse. The place still exists, but the moment is gone. His childhood, his family, his belonging—these happened here once, but they do not exist here now. They exist only in his memory, and memory is not a location. It is portable after all. He carries it with him. It lives nowhere but in him.

This is what return teaches: you cannot go back. You can only go to where back used to be.

By the lake, the rain is steady now. The water no longer reflects anything—the surface is too disturbed, too broken by impact.

He understands: the loss was not of home but of the illusion that home is a place; That it waits for you; That it forgives your leaving by welcoming your return.

Home is not a place. It is a relation. And relations change. The people change. You change. The threads that bound you together loosen, fray, break. You can visit the location, but the relation is gone.

The mystic has no home. This is not a tragedy. This is a necessity. To see clearly, you must stand outside. But outside has no location. You cannot return to inside once you have learned to see from out here.

The philosopher has no home, because thought itself is the only homeland of the awake. There was no banishment. Only participation. Only the endless circulation of self, through self.

He thought he was exiled. But exile implies a home you can return to, a place you were cast out from. What he has learned: there was no casting out. There was only leaving, and staying left, and discovering that "there" and "here" are both words for elsewhere.

Perhaps this is what all the reductions were preparing him for. Not to find home but to accept homelessness. Not as a lack but as a condition.

The lake, like a patient mirror, holds it all—the journey, the loss, the return that is not return, the endless becoming of what cannot arrive.

# VIII

The rain withdraws. Light returns in fragments —shards upon the trembling lake. Each glimmer is a thought surrendering its edge. The lake is not glass anymore. The surface moves, unsettled, carrying the memory of disturbance.

He is sixty-four when he finishes the work.

Years of thinking, writing, revising. The systematic philosophy: how consciousness arises within reality, not apart from it. How the observer and observed are mutually constituting. How being is relational, processual, and participatory. How everything connects to everything else in webs of relation that have no outside, no standing apart, no view from nowhere.

He doesn't know what he would work on next. What he couldn't say: I need to know if it was worth it.

The philosophy explains all of it. Why his mother's tears were not external to his choice, but the substance of it. Why assimilation required subtraction. Why science taught him to see through complexity to mechanism, and why that vision, while true, was insufficient. Why solitude became his mode of being. Why his children carry none of his weight and are freer for it. Why his name became dangerous and why distance did not protect him. Why home is not a place but a relation, and why all relations change.

The philosophy explains. But does it console? Does it offer peace?

The young man at the airport thought he was choosing knowledge that would save something. The family. The country. Himself. He was wrong on all counts. The knowledge did not save anything. It explained. Explanation is not salvation.

The philosophy says: all your choices led here necessarily. You could not have been other than what you became.

But necessity is not comfort. The philosophy explains why his mother cried, but it does not dry her tears. It explains why the tradition died with him, but it does not resurrect it. It explains why he belongs nowhere completely, but it does not give him a home.

Would he choose this again, knowing what it cost?

The philosophy says: you did not choose. You participated in choosing. The choice chose itself through you, through circumstances, through relations you did not create but could not escape.

All the choices led here. To this lake, this moment, this recognition. The solitary man contemplating a life lived in fragments, understanding finally the pattern of the fragmentation, but not made whole by the understanding.

The mystic withdraws into deeper reality. But what if the deeper reality is just more clarity about how alone you are? What if participation, fully understood, means recognizing that you are connected to everything but at home in nothing?

Perhaps this is what he came to learn. That there is no final consolation. No moment when understanding makes the cost worthwhile. No philosophy that erases the tears, the broken lineage, the permanent displacement.

Perhaps the philosophy itself is what he made from the wreckage. Not compensation. Not justification. Just—the thing he could make. The only thing.

The lake is still now. Different from how it began, but still. The leaves have decided—some falling, some holding on a while longer. Autumn deepening. The season is turning.

He came to think about nothing. Nothing became everything. Everything became this: a man by a lake, understanding what his life cost and what it built, knowing that understanding is not the same as peace, but having no other answer.

Was it worth it?

He does not know. But he is still here. Still participating. Still engaged with reality in the only way he knows—through solitude, through thought, through the recognition that you cannot step outside to answer such questions. You can only continue. The choice continues choosing itself through you, and you call this living.

He does not need the answer anymore.

He has become the asking.

The question remains.

If he could go back, knowing everything:
*Would he board that plane?*

SEA

# THE SEA
## DOES NOT CARE

## Pre-Dawn

Four-thirty: neither night nor morning, that temporal membrane where circadian certainty falters. His waking is not arrival but continuation—consciousness emerging from metabolic slowness into a darkness, which is not the Northern cities' darkness.

Sound announces what light withholds. The sea's breathing, arterial and venous, systolic compression and diastolic release—not metaphor but structural homology. Through closed shutters, through concrete and plaster, through the medium of air itself, the Mediterranean performs its existence without witness. The baker's motorcycle coughs to life three streets away. A cat disturbs something metallic in the alley. Alexandria's pre-dawn orchestra tunes itself according to no conductor, each instrument entering when internal necessity dictates.

He does not turn on the lights. The phosphorescent numerals of his watch—radium-226 decaying with its half-life of sixteen hundred years—provide the only visible certainty. Time measured by atomic deterioration, entropy made useful. His feet sense the floor's temperature, fourteen degrees cooler than the body's core, thermal gradients establishing themselves according to laws that precede consciousness and will outlast it. To dress in darkness is to discover clothing's phenomenology stripped of visual confirmation. The shirt was recently purchased from a shop whose proprietor spoke an Arabic accelerated beyond his dormant comprehension.

The door's lock mechanism—pin tumbler design, invented in ancient Egypt, releases with metallic certainty. The hallway's darkness differs from the apartment's: communal, traversed, carrying traces of neighbours he hasn't met.

Three floors descended, each landing a pause in gravitational negotiation. Architecture as arrested flow—the building settling into its foundations with barely perceptible adjustments, Portland cement's calcium silicates frozen mid-reaction, permanent but not eternal. The street door opens onto what he imagined as the philosophical city of Alexandria, before actual Alexandria wakes.

East. The cardinal direction chosen not by decision but by something prior to choice. The kind of knowledge the body harbours below consciousness. He walks toward where the sun will appear, but it has not yet announced itself toward where the Mediterranean curves away from Africa toward Asia, toward waters that have been wine-dark and rosy-fingered. Simply water, the accumulation of hydrogen and oxygen molecules held in a liquid state by temperature and pressure conditions specific to this planet's distance from its star.

The Corniche reveals itself through tactile and olfactory intelligence. Salt's crystalline presence, sodium chloride in aerosol suspension, deposits itself on the lips, accumulates in the nasal passages, and infiltrates the lungs with each inhalation. The sea's chemistry written in air: not just salt but sulphur compounds from algae, trace metals from three continents' erosion, hydrocarbons from yesterday's fishing boats. The smell is not memory—memory would be representation, mediation—but direct molecular encounter, olfactory receptors binding to specific compounds, electrochemical signals racing along cranial nerve one to the limbic system, where emotion and memory interweave below the threshold of language.

His feet find the sea wall's edge through proprioceptive calculation, the body's knowledge of its own position in space. Limestone blocks quarried from Tura, the same source as the pyramids, though these nineteenth-century installments lack their ancestors' precision. The stone is still warm from yesterday's solar collection, thermal mass releasing photon-gifted energy back to the cooler air. He places both palms flat against the stone, feeling its granular texture, calcium carbonate skeletons of marine organisms compressed over geological time into this solid that pretends permanence while slowly dissolving, molecule by molecule, back into the sea that made it.

The Mediterranean's sound here is not singular but multiple: waves against stone, water withdrawing over shingle, the deeper percussion of swells meeting the continental shelf. Each wave's acoustic signature is unique, unrepeatable, though the pattern persists. Frequency and amplitude encode information about wind speed, fetch distance, and seafloor topography. The sea speaks in languages older than human speech, older than vertebrate evolution, the dialogue between water and shore that began when Earth's surface cooled enough to permit liquid's existence.

Behind him, the city's electrical grid maintains its hum, alternating current flowing through copper arteries, resistance generating heat, entropy tax paid on civilization's luminous ambitions. Street lights—high-pressure sodium lamps emitting their characteristic yellow—create pools of visibility that paradoxically deepen the surrounding darkness. But he stands beyond their reach, in the liminal zone where artificial illumination surrenders to its absence.

The sea neither awaits nor anticipates, yet its waiting is its work. This thought arrives unbidden, the kind of formation that emerges from the interface between consciousness and its environment. He reaches for the notebook in his pocket—leather-bound, pages cream-colored though invisible now, purchased from the same shop as the shirt. The fountain pen's weight is familiar in fingers that have written countless reports, diagnostic assessments, where precision saves lives or confirms their conclusion. But here, in darkness, writing becomes purely kinesthetic, trust in the hand's learned patterns, muscle memory of letter formation.

Process without a witness remains process. The circulation continues whether observed or not, blood through vessels, currents through waters, thoughts through neural networks. To stand before the invisible sea is to confront epistemology's limits: what can be known without light? Everything essential. The wave-function doesn't collapse until measurement, but the waves themselves collapse continuously against this shore, measured by stone's erosion, by the salt crystallizing on my skin, by the pressure variations in my cochlea. I am not observing the sea. We are co-constituting this moment, this interface, this participation.

The pen stops. To write philosophy in darkness is to trust that patterns persist and ink's molecular bonds with cellulose will hold until photons permit their reading.

East, the horizon remains indistinguishable from the sea, darkness uniform but not undifferentiated. The eye's rods, more sensitive than cones, detect variations in what seems uniformly dark. Scotopic vision, they called it in medical school, from the Greek skotos, darkness. Twenty minutes required for rhodopsin regeneration, the eye's chemistry adapting to darkness as blood chemistry adapts to altitude, as gut bacteria adapt to diet, as the sea itself adapts to temperature, salinity, and the Nile's seasonal contributions.

A fisherman passes, invisible except for his cigarette's ember and the plastic bucket's scrape against pavement. They don't speak—what language would suffice? Arabic, which Hakim once knew but now knows he doesn't? English, which would mark him as foreign? French, Alexandria's colonial ghost language? Silence serves better, acknowledging co-presence without demanding communication. The fisherman continues west, toward the harbour, toward boats that will venture out before light, reading the sea through sonar, GPS, technologies that exceed human senses while remaining extensions of them.

The first grey. Not yet light but light's rumour, the eastern sky's density shifting, becoming less opaque. The transition is not sudden but proceeds by infinitesimal gradations, like a fever breaking, like consciousness emerging from anesthesia. The horizon begins to declare itself, a line dividing two darknesses, sea from sky, though the division is cognitive projection, atmosphere and hydrosphere interfacing without boundary, water vapour rising, condensing, precipitating, the planet's circulatory system operating at scales from molecular to global.

He remains standing, waiting without expectation, or rather with expectation stripped of specific content. The sea will become visible—this much is certain. But which sea? The Mediterranean of classical antiquity, wine-dark, Homeric, travelled by Phoenicians who invented the alphabet to track commercial transactions, an abstraction born from commerce? The Arab Sea, Bahr al-Rum, the Roman Sea that outlasted Rome? The contemporary sea, warming, acidifying, its fish populations collapsing, its waters carrying microplastics that enter food chains, that accumulate in tissues, that will outlast the civilizations that produced them?

All these seas. None of them. The sea is a process, not a product; circulation, not a container.

> Before dawn, blood circulates unseen through vessels mapped but not transparent. The doctor knows without seeing: here the carotid, here the jugular, here the subclavian artery. Knowledge through palpation, through pressure, through the pulse that announces hydraulic certainty. The sea's pulse against this stone is not metaphorical correspondence but structural echo—fluid dynamics operating at different scales, same mathematics governing both flows. To feel one is to understand the other. This is not an analogy but homology.

The notebook closes. The darkness continues its slow dissolution. Alexandria stirs—a door opening, a motor starting, a child's cry from an upper window immediately hushed. The city's metabolic rate increases, ATP hydrolysis accelerating in millions of cells in thousands of bodies beginning their day's labour. Hakim turns east, toward the light that has not yet arrived but whose arrival is encoded in the planet's rotation, in the solar system's architecture, in the cosmos's expansion from its original singularity, all of history contracted into this moment of waiting for dawn over the Mediterranean, which doesn't wait but continues its processes indifferent to observation, though observation changes everything, always has.

# DAWN

Grey admits colour gradually, reluctantly, as if skeptical of its own spectrum. Five-thirty and walking east along the Corniche, He moves through air that carries yesterday's heat in thermal pockets, zones where temperature varies by degrees that skin registers but consciousness barely notes. The sea to his left remains more heard than seen, though seeing has begun its uncertain establishment. Not yet the Mediterranean's notorious blue but a grey that contains blue's possibility, as RNA contains protein's possibility, as the fertilized cell contains the organism's entire future, potential waiting for conditions that permit expression.

The horizon sharpens. Where before was undifferentiated darkness, now emerges the line that philosophy has contemplated since philosophy began contemplating: the boundary that is not boundary, the division that connects what it divides. Sea meeting sky, or sky meeting sea, the prepositions revealing their inadequacy. They don't meet—they *inter-are*, to use a Buddhist formulation that participatory process monism would recognize, though recognition across traditions is always translation, always transformation, never simple equivalence.

Light's epistemology reveals itself in stages. First, the discrimination of forms: this is a building, that is a tree, there is the sea wall's edge. Then texture: the water's surface is not uniform but structured by waves, each catching dawn light differently, creating patterns that exist only in this specific angular relationship between observer, surface, and sun still below the horizon. Then colour, emerging not all at once but sequentially, as if the visible spectrum remembers its own order, red wavelengths first, seven hundred nanometers, then orange, yellow, the others waiting their turn.

A fisherman prepares his boat, the same or a different fisherman from before—in this light, individual identity remains uncertain. The boat is small, painted blue like every fishing boat on this coast, as if the sea demands chromatic harmony from those who would harvest it. The man works with practiced efficiency, movements economical, each gesture necessary, nothing wasted. This is knowledge incarnate: not theory but practice, not abstract but embodied, the kind of knowing that comes only from repetition, from participation, from submitting to the sea's teaching, which is not kind but is consistent.

The sun approaches. Not visible yet, but announced by the eastern sky's inflammation, red-orange spreading like a histological stain revealing cellular structure. The comparison arrives—eosin and hematoxylin, the dyes that make cells visible under microscopy, that reveal what light alone cannot show. Dawn is a diagnostic tool, revealing the day's potential. The sky's colour intensifies, deepens, and suddenly—though suddenly is wrong, the process being continuous—the sun's edge breaches the horizon.

The moment resists description even as it demands it. Every dawn is structurally identical—the planet's rotation bringing this longitude into solar exposure—and every dawn is unique—this cloud configuration, this atmospheric condition, this observer. Heraclitus: The sun is new every day. Literally true, the sun's fusion processes ensure that today's photons differ from yesterday's, though the pattern persists. Eight minutes and twenty seconds those photons travelled, the speed of light through vacuum being constant, to arrive at this retina, these rhodopsin molecules, this consciousness that transforms electromagnetic radiation into meaning.

The sea begins its chromatic transformation. Grey yields to silver as the angle of incidence shifts, as wavelengths segregate according to their energies. The water is not blue—water is colourless—but water in sufficient depth absorbs red wavelengths, reflects blue, creates the appearance that language solidifies into identity: the blue Mediterranean. But now, in dawn's light, it is not blue but a complexity that language fails to specify: silver-gold-grey with undertones of green where algae concentrate, purple where depth increases, white where waves break, each colour a function of physics, chemistry, biology, observation angle, and cognitive processing.

Hakim watches the sun climb, its movement

imperceptible moment to moment but obvious across minutes. The Earth rotates at roughly one thousand miles per hour at this latitude, but the sensation is stillness. Motion relative to what? The question physics answers mathematically, but philosophy continues to probe.

A young woman passes, hijab bright green, smartphone in hand, earbuds delivering private sound into her consciousness. She doesn't see him, doesn't see the sea, her attention absorbed by the screen's mediation. This, too, is Alexandria: not the ancient city of libraries and lighthouses but the contemporary city of five million, of unemployment, of young people planning emigration even as they walk along the Corniche their grandparents walked. She pauses, removes one earbud, takes a selfie with the sunrise behind her, and posts it to a platform that currently carries identity performances across networks. The image will circulate, accumulate likes, become data, contribute to algorithms that shape what others see, what becomes visible, and what remains dark.

> Light enables sight but also blinds. These sunrise photographs proliferating across networks—do they document dawn or replace it? The image is more real than the experience, the documentation preceding the event it documents.

The light is changing again, gold yielding to white as

the sun climbs higher. The sea's blue begins asserting itself, dozens of blues, hundreds, each wave face its own shade, the colour constantly reconstituting itself like blood cells constantly renewed, the body maintaining itself through controlled death and rebirth, apoptosis and regeneration in balance.

A coffee vendor has established operations, the equipment minimal—gas burner, pot, cups, sugar—but sufficient. Hakim orders and drinks, watching the harbour reveal itself in strengthening light: fishing boats returning from night work, cargo ships awaiting permission to dock, yachts of the wealthy who weekend here, escaping Cairo's density for the coast's relative openness.

"You are Egyptian?" the vendor asks, though the question carries doubt.

"Yes, originally," Hakim answers, though yes simplifies, Egyptian has meant different things across his lifetime—Nasser's Arab socialism, Sadat's opening, Mubarak's stagnation, the revolution that failed or succeeded or both, depending on what one measures.

"But living outside," the vendor continues, not question but diagnosis, reading something in Hakim's posture, his clothes, his manner of holding the cup.

"Canada," Hakim concedes.

"Ah." The sound contains multitudes—envy, dismissal, understanding, incomprehension. The conversation ends. Other customers arrive. The day's commerce begins.

Hakim walks further east, the sun now climbing rapidly, or apparently rapidly. The Earth's rotation is constant, but our perception of it varies with attention, with the day's tasks, and with age. Children experience time dilated, stretched, each day containing eternities. Age compresses, accelerates, years passing like months once passed. Time's arrow—entropy manifesting in both subjective consciousness and universal expansion, the same directionality expressed at different scales. The universe's temperature declines asymptotically toward absolute zero, approachable but never reached.

The Corniche fills slowly with others: joggers whose footfalls establish rhythm, elderly men with prayer beads whose fingers establish a different rhythm, women in groups whose conversations establish social rhythm. Alexandria waking, though waking suggests prior sleep and cities never sleep, only shift, only modulate, their consciousness distributed across millions of nodes, no central processor, no unified experience.

Looking back west, he can see how far he's walked— three kilometres, maybe four. The city spreads along the coast, apartment buildings of varying decay, some Ottoman, some colonial French, some Nasser-era concrete, some recent glass and steel, attempting Dubai's aesthetic without Dubai's capital. Layers of history coexisting uneasily, each era's ambitions partially realized, partially ruined. Like sedimentary rock, like tree rings, like the archaeological tells that dot this landscape, civilization accumulates vertically, each generation building on the previous' s rubble.

The sun is fully established now, its authority undeniable. Shadows sharpen, shorten, and will continue shortening until noon, when they nearly disappear, only to lengthen again toward evening. The day's arc is predictable, has been predicted since humans began observing patterns, recognizing cycles, creating calendars that are time made spatial, duration given form.

> The dawn is complete, but dawn is never complete, always occurring somewhere as the Earth rotates, as the terminator—that line dividing day from night—sweeps westward at fifteen degrees longitude per hour. While I watched this dawn, others watched it from Crete, from Sicily, from the Balearics, the same sun from different angles, the same process differently witnessed. The Mediterranean doesn't experience dawn—it is the medium through which dawn is experienced, the surface that reflects, refracts, and makes visible what would otherwise be abstract celestial mechanics.

He closes the notebook, returns it to his pocket, where

it travels with him like memory made material, like thought given weight. The pen, too, returns to its place, ink diminished by some millilitres, words extracted from liquid, meaning from matter. Neurons firing, synapses connecting, electrochemical cascades that are consciousness or produce consciousness or are produced by consciousness—the hard problem that philosophy hasn't solved, that perhaps cannot be solved from within consciousness. The eye is unable to see itself seeing.

A final look at the sea before turning back toward the city proper. It is fully blue now, that particular Mediterranean blue that is not the Atlantic's blue or the Pacific's blue or any lake's blue, but this blue, specific to this basin, this latitude, this mineral content, this history of seeing. Homer saw it wine-dark, perhaps at sunset, perhaps with eyes that parsed the spectrum differently, perhaps with language that categorized colour according to different principles. We see it blue and cannot see it otherwise, blue encoded in our expectations, our postcards, our memories, real and inherited.

The fisherman from earlier passes, his boat returning. "Good catch?" Hakim asks. "The sea was generous," the fisherman responds, the sea's generosity measured not in absolute catch but in the relationship between effort and reward, between risk and return. The fisherman continues toward wherever fish are sold, weighed, purchased, transformed from sea's gift to market's commodity. The economics of it: price per kilogram fluctuating with supply, demand, season, the invisible hand that Adam Smith imagined moving markets but which is really millions of visible hands exchanging currency for calories, for protein, for the taste of the sea on the tongue, salt and iodine and the particular sweetness of fresh fish that is not sweetness but its own category, umami before the Japanese named it, savory satisfaction that predates language.

Hakim walks back toward his apartment, toward the day that dawn has initiated but not determined. The streets are fuller now, Cairo's overflow, Alexandria's year-round residents, tourists beginning their documented adventures. Languages multiply: Arabic in its various dialects, English from the hotels, Russian from the new money, French from the old associations, Italian from those whose grandparents stayed when others left. The Mediterranean's linguistic diversity, Babel's legacy, or Babel's gift—the multiplication that prevents unity but enables diversity, that makes translation necessary, that keeps meaning in motion.

The sun climbs higher. The day heats. The sea continues its work of evaporation, condensation, and circulation. Somewhere, rain falls that was Mediterranean water, will be again. Somewhere, rivers flow toward this basin, carrying sediment, nutrients, pollutants, and history. The Nile, the Ebro, the Rhône, the Po—each contributing its particular chemistry, its particular story, to the sea that receives all, mixes all, returns all transformed.

Dawn is over, but not yet. Not this dawn. This dawn continues in its effects—the warmth that will build through the day, the light that will enable photosynthesis, vision, the reading of notebooks written in darkness, the interpretation of words that gesture toward meaning that exceeds language, that participates in the world's becoming while attempting to understand it.

The apartment building's entrance is shade, coolness, respite. Three flights up, reversing the morning's descent, feeling in his legs the labour that gravity demands, the work of lifting mass against acceleration, potential energy accumulating with each step. The door opens to the unfamiliar space, yesterday's arrival still fresh, still estranging. But something has shifted. The dawn walk has begun something—not transformation, too grand a word, but adjustment, calibration, the beginning of participation in Alexandria's rhythm, which is not his rhythm but might become the rhythm they create together, the pattern that emerges from their mutual engagement.

He sits at the small table on the balcony that faces the sea. From here, elevated, the Mediterranean spreads to the horizon, that line he stood before in darkness, now visible, now ordinary, now extraordinary again if attention permits, if the mind doesn't habituate, doesn't assume, doesn't take dawn for granted simply because it comes daily.

The notebook opens to the pages written in darkness. The words are legible, mostly, though some lines wander, overlap, and create palimpsests that require interpretation. This, too, is appropriate—thought capturing itself imperfectly, meaning exceeding its inscription, the process continuing beyond its documentation.

> Mediterranean dawn. Not possessive but participatory. I didn't observe the dawn—I participated in it, contributed my consciousness to its occurrence, was changed by it in ways I'm still discovering. The fisherman knew this, knew that the sea's generosity isn't separate from his attention to it, his skill in reading it, his submission to its patterns. Knowledge as participation, not extraction.

> Tomorrow there will be another dawn. I won't see it—I'll participate in it or not, will be conscious or sleeping, will be alive or not, eventually not, certainly not. But the dawn doesn't require me. It requires only the Earth's rotation, the sun's combustion, and the atmosphere's mediation. My participation is contingent, temporary, and grateful. The

process includes me today, will exceed me tomorrow or eventually tomorrow. This is not loss but location—finding one's place in processes larger than oneself, processes that were before consciousness, that will be after.

The pen stops. The morning is fully established. From the balcony, the Mediterranean has achieved its full blue, though full is always partial, though blue is always approximate, though achievement is always process, never product.

Time to close the notebook. Time to enter the day that dawn has made possible. Time to walk again, to participate again, to allow the city and sea to work their slow transformation on consciousness.

# MORNING

Seven o'clock and the apartment has become a provisional shelter, its walls suddenly constrictive, the furniture suggesting domesticity that participatory consciousness cannot accept, not yet. The morning demands movement, not the dawn's tentative exploration but purposeful traversal, the city requiring witness at its full metabolic expression.

Hakim descends again—west this time, against the sun's trajectory, into light rather than following it. The reversal is not arbitrary; consciousness seeks what it hasn't yet encountered, the harbour leftward. The Corniche continues its arc, that limestone boundary between terrestrial and marine.

The city's morning metabolism expresses itself in diesel exhaust and bread scent, in the metallic percussion of shutters rising, in the polyphonic negotiation of traffic where lanes are suggestions rather than prescriptions. A different Alexandria than dawn revealed—not contemplative but commercial, not potential but kinetic. The transformation is not merely temporal but ontological: the city that exists for consciousness at rest differs from the city that exists for consciousness in motion. Though *exists* is wrong, suggesting stability where there is only *process*.

He passes the Bibliotheca Alexandrina, that

architectural assertion of recovered heritage, its disc-like structure tilted toward the Mediterranean as if listening for whispers from its drowned predecessor. Eleven floors, seven of them below ground—a building that burrows rather than soars, seeking foundation rather than elevation. The ancient library had no such architectural ambition. It was simply rooms, storage, the technology of papyrus and parchment, requiring no special environment beyond dryness and darkness when not being read. This new iteration, opened in 2002, attempts to materialize memory, to give form to absence, to make present what is irretrievably past.

> The Library that burned—if it burned, the stories multiply and contradict—contained, they say, Aristotle's personal collection, the complete works of Aeschylus, Sophocles' 123 dramas of which we possess seven. Knowledge as commodity, hoarded, vulnerable to flame, to flood, to the simple entropy of organic molecules surrendering their bonds. But also: knowledge as pattern, surviving its material substrate. We have Euclid's Elements not from his hand but from copies of copies, each transmission introducing errors that become features, mutations that enable evolution. The new library cannot recover the old library's

scrolls, but can continue its project—gathering, organizing, preserving, though preserving what? Not information, which proliferates beyond any institution's capacity. Perhaps preserving the idea of preservation itself.

Two tourists photograph themselves against the library's tilted wall, their poses practiced, immediate review on phone screens, deletion and repetition until the image satisfies some internal criterion. They speak German, or Swiss German, where the consonants are differently weighted. They don't enter the building—the photograph suffices, presence documented, Alexandria added to their collection of places possessed through images. Hakim, too, doesn't enter, but for different reasons, or perhaps the same reason differently articulated. To enter would be to accept the building's claim to continuity, its architectural argument that something persists across the centuries of absence. Better to pass, to acknowledge without affirming, to let the library exist in peripheral vision where it belongs, margin rather than center.

The harbour area begins to announce itself through olfactory gradient—salt concentration increasing, diesel mixing with marine decay, that particular combination that every working port produces, that globalizes the local even as it localizes the global. Container ships rest at anchor, their names declaring origins.

The ancient harbour lies beneath these waters, Cleopatra's palace among the submerged structures, though Cleopatra is a convenient designation for complex archaeological stratification. Marine archaeologists have mapped the ruins using sonar, photogrammetry, and technologies that reveal without exposing, that maintain the water's protective custody. Better preserved submerged than exposed to air, to tourism, to the particular violence of making the past present for consumption.

A café presents itself, or rather Hakim's trajectory intersects with its location, the encounter appearing inevitable retrospectively, though contingency governed each turn. Plastic chairs, aluminum tables, the universal furniture of provisional gathering. The proprietor is perhaps sixty, perhaps seventy, age becoming indefinite after certain thresholds, the body marking time differently, accumulated damage creating individual chronology. Hakim orders coffee—the man offers Nescafé, globalization's gift to caffeine delivery, instant satisfaction for those who accept approximation as equivalent.

"You are Egyptian?" the proprietor asks, the question becoming familiar, identity requiring constant verification.

"Originally," Hakim responds, originally containing both truth and evasion.

"But not currently," the man observes, not accusation

but diagnosis.

"Canadian," Hakim concedes, though Canadian explains nothing, explains everything wrongly.

"The brain drain," the proprietor says in English, the phrase itself English, no Arabic equivalent carrying the same resignation mixed with pride—Egypt produces minds worthy of draining, even as their drainage diminishes what remains.

The coffee arrives, foam thick enough to support sugar briefly before molecular forces overcome structural integrity. Through the café's frame—it lacks walls, only posts supporting a corrugated roof—the Harbour curves, fishing boats returning though it's early still for their second departure. The two-cycle rhythm: pre-dawn for deep-water fish, late morning for different species, different depths, the sea stratified vertically as the city is stratified socially, each zone its own ecosystem, own rules, own possibilities.

A young woman enters, or appears—her movement too fluid for entry's mechanics. Perhaps twenty-five, lab coat over jeans, the costume of scientific authority adapted to contemporary casual. She orders in rapid Arabic, takes a table nearby, opens a laptop whose screen displays what Hakim recognizes as sequence data—the four-letter alphabet of nucleotides, ATCG, in combinations that encode existence.

"RNA sequencing?" he asks in English, the technical term lacking an Arabic equivalent, or rather, the Arabic would be translation, not native terminology.

She looks up, evaluates, and decides. "DNA, actually. Environmental sampling from the harbour." Her English carries British inflection overlaid on an Egyptian foundation, education's palimpsest.

"Marine biology?"

"Microbiology. We're mapping bacterial populations, how they've changed since—" she pauses, searching for euphemism or deciding against it, "—since the sewage treatment failures."

The conversation that follows is technical, professional, the kind of exchange that transcends nationality through shared vocabulary and methodology. She's studying at Alexandria University, her project traces antibiotic resistance genes through marine environments, the harbour as a reservoir for genetic innovation, bacteria exchanging plasmids like ideas, and horizontal gene transfer enabling rapid adaptation.

"The Mediterranean is becoming a super-bacterial breeding ground," she explains, her tone clinical rather than alarmed. "Antibiotics from agricultural runoff, from human waste, from aquaculture—they create selective pressure. The bacteria that survive are increasingly resistant. We're watching evolution in real-time."

Evolution in real-time. The phrase lodges in consciousness, demands examination. Darwin imagined deep time, geological patience, and changes imperceptible within a human lifetime. But bacteria, with their twenty-minute generations, compress evolution into observable spans. The harbour she studies is not the harbour of last year, microbiologically speaking. Its bacterial population has adapted, incorporated new genes, and developed new resistances. Process philosophy made literal—identity through transformation, pattern persisting through material exchange.

"Like cancer," Hakim offers, his own expertise surfacing. "Leukemic cells evolving resistance to chemotherapy. The treatment creates selective pressure; the resistant clones proliferate."

"Exactly," she agrees, then pauses. "You're medical?"

"Was. Am." The tense confusion is accurate—he is credentialed, experienced, but not currently practicing, the knowledge persistent but dormant, like spores awaiting favourable conditions.

They discuss the parallel: blood as ecosystem, cancer as evolution, treatment as environmental pressure. The conversation ranges through molecular biology, evolutionary dynamics, and the philosophy of medicine, though neither names it as such. She mentions Canguilhem—*The Normal and the Pathological*—and he recognizes a kindred intelligence, someone who thinks beyond their discipline's boundaries, who recognizes those boundaries as provisional, porous.

"The fishermen hate our research," she mentions, gesturing toward the harbour. "We document what they don't want documented—the contamination, the declining fish stocks. They think we're bad for business."

"Are you?"

"Truth is bad for business if business depends on denial." She closes the laptop, preparing to leave. "But the sea doesn't care about business. It continues its processes. The bacteria adapt. The fish populations crash or recover. The chemistry changes. We just document, try to understand patterns."

She leaves without a formal goodbye, with scientific abruptness that assumes an ongoing conversation rather than a conclusion. Hakim remains, watches the harbour's morning commerce—boats departing and arriving, nets being repaired, the ancient rhythms persisting despite or through contemporary disruptions.

> Knowledge circulates or stagnates. The ancient library accumulated. Modern science reverses this, generates data faster than comprehension, and produces information that exceeds interpretation. The young scientist documents bacterial evolution, but what does it mean? The patterns she detects are real—genes spreading, resistance developing—but the pattern is not purpose. Evolution has no telos, no direction, only a response to pressure. The Mediterranean becomes a reservoir for resistance genes—so? The bacteria don't care.

The sea doesn't care. Only consciousness cares, and consciousness is a recent addition, perhaps temporary, certainly not necessary for the processes to continue.

A swimmer appears, unexpected at this hour, at this location—not the tourist beaches eastward but here among the working boats, the diesel slicks, the documented contamination. An older man, perhaps Hakim's age, entering the water with practiced economy, no hesitation at temperature or chemistry. He swims parallel to shore, steady crawl, breathing rhythm synchronized with stroke, the body's mechanics refined through repetition into something approaching efficiency, though efficiency in water is always relative, humans being terrestrial adaptations momentarily returning to ancestral medium.

The swimmer continues, perhaps half a kilometre, then returns, emerges, towels himself with the same economy that marked entry. He notices Hakim watching, "You swim?" the man asks, though the question carries invitation rather than inquiry.

"Not here." The qualification acknowledges the possibility without commitment.

"The water is polluted, they say. Bacteria, heavy metals, microplastics." The man towels his hair, casual about contamination. "But I've been swimming here for twenty-five years. My body and the harbour have reached accommodation. We've evolved together."

The statement carries scientific precision despite conversational delivery. Evolution, accommodation—the vocabulary suggests education beyond casual usage.

"You're visiting?" the swimmer asks, reading something in Hakim's observational stance, his particular quality of attention.

"Recently arrived." The explanation invites further query.

"For work? Research?" the man asks.

"Something like that." Hakim's response is both accurate and evasive.

"I teach mathematics," the swimmer adds. "Secondary school, here in Alexandria. Though mathematics is philosophy by other means—patterns, relationships, the structures that persist through transformation."

They shake hands. "You came to Alexandria specifically, not Cairo, where opportunities are, Alexandria—the city of departure, nostalgia. Why?"

"The philosophical tradition," Hakim offers.

"The mythology," the man interrupts, not unkindly. "Everyone comes for the mythology. Foreigners seeking the cosmopolitan past, Egyptians seeking escape from the present. Both disappointed."

A pause while a delivery truck passes, diesel exhaust thick. Both men wait without covering faces, accepting the air as they accept the water.

"You chose to come," the man says. "That's different

from returning. Those who return seek what was. Those who choose seek what might be. The distinction matters."

"And those who stay?"

"We seek nothing. We simply continue. Teaching mathematics to children who will leave, swimming in water that worsens, watching the city proceed through its processes. It's not resignation—it's participation without illusion."

They discuss the paradox—Hakim chose Alexandria for its philosophical significance, but the man remains despite its philosophical emptiness. One seeks meaning in a city that's become pure process, the other continues process in a city drained of meaning.

"The students I teach, they dream of Europe, anywhere but here. How to explain that Alexandria teaches through its failures what success cannot—that entropy is as philosophical as construction, that decline reveals structures, growth conceals?"

"You make it sound like a conscious choice rather than a circumstance."

"Everything is circumstance reframed as choice, or choice revealed as circumstance. The distinction collapses in practice." He mounts a bicycle and cycles away.

Hakim continues westward, but the encounter has shifted something. Not recognition of shared past but acknowledgment of different relationships to the same present. The teacher participates through repetition, Hakim through observation. Both are valid methods of engaging processes that include consciousness.

Walking now with different attention—not seeking what he'd read and imagined about Alexandria but observing what Alexandria has become. The contemporary city that continues despite scholarly projection, that offers no validation for philosophical fantasy, that processes contamination and consciousness with equal indifference.

> Persistence through repetition, not progress. The phrase articulates something essential about place, about staying, about the difference between those who leave and those who remain. Hakim sought progress—medical advancement, career trajectory, and the immigrant's faith in transformation. The teacher accepted repetition—teaching the children, swimming in progressively polluted water, watching Alexandria simultaneously decay and develop. Neither choice is superior, but they produce different consciousnesses, different relationships to time and to change.

Walking westward still, the sun now high enough to create sharp shadows, the morning's gold light whitening toward noon's harsh illumination. The harbour continues its arc, industrial facilities replacing fishing boats, the scale shifting from artisanal to corporate. Cranes load containers with mechanical precision, the global supply chain's local node, goods from China trans-shipping to Europe, African raw materials heading toward Asian processing, the circulation that capitalism calls efficiency, but which is really entropy accelerated, resources converted to waste via commodity.

He thinks of blood's circulation, that metaphor that is not a metaphor but a structural echo. Arterial blood carries oxygen, nutrients, toward tissues that consume, that produce waste, that return venous blood depleted, requiring pulmonary renewal, cardiac propulsion, the cycle continuing until it doesn't. The global economy circulates similarly—resources extracted, processed, consumed, discarded, the waste accumulating in places like this harbour, in futures like the young scientist documents without judgment, with clinical precision that masks or reveals despair.

A vendor offers fish, this morning's catch displayed on ice that melts steadily, entropy made visible. The fish are small—no large predators anymore, those populations collapsed from overfishing, only the species that reproduce quickly, that adapt to disruption. Ecological simplification, diversity surrendering to resilience, or what appears as resilience but might be system failure's early stage. The vendor calls prices, reduces them as Hakim passes without stopping, the commerce of necessity, selling before spoilage, before the ice becomes water, before the morning's harvest becomes afternoon's waste.

The Mediterranean as an ecosystem is dying, has been dying since humans began concentrating along its shores, will continue dying until it doesn't, until it transforms into something else, some other configuration of chemistry and biology. Death is transformation, not termination. The ancient library died, but knowledge continued elsewhere. The Roman Empire died, but Latin persisted in evolved forms. Species die, but their genes continue in descendants or don't, ending being as real as continuance. Process philosophy accommodates both—not everything persists, not every pattern continues. Some processes conclude. The difficulty is distinguishing conclusion from transformation while still within the process.

Noon approaches, and the heat is building toward its daily maximum. The morning walk has covered perhaps six kilometres, a trivial distance globally but significant locally, each meter carrying specific history, specific possibility. The harbour curves back toward the Corniche, toward the apartment, though return is not retreat but completion of circuit, the path that enables comprehension of territory, that transforms space into place through embodied knowledge.

Near the Corniche's resumption, where the harbour yields to open sea, a small group has gathered around something invisible from a distance. Approaching, Hakim discovers a sea turtle, dead, washed ashore during the night. *Caretta caretta*, the loggerhead, once common here, is now endangered, this individual's death adding to population statistics that trend toward zero. The turtle is perhaps a meter long, mass maybe thirty kilograms, the shell intact but flesh beginning decomposition's work, bacteria and heat collaborating in material recycling.

A child asks why it died. The mother responds with comforting fiction—old age, natural causes. But visible plastic emerges from the throat, a bag or wrapper that mimics jellyfish in water, that turtles consume, that blocks digestion, that kills slowly through starvation, while the stomach fills with petroleum products. The child doesn't see or doesn't understand the plastic's significance. The mother sees, understands, and chooses silence's mercy.

Someone calls authorities—the turtle will be removed, disposed of, its death becoming a statistic if recorded, anecdote if not. The crowd disperses, the morning's rhythm resuming, the incident already becoming memory, story, the turtle transformed from biological entity to narrative element, its material existence concluded but its symbolic presence just beginning, rippling through consciousness like waves through water, each witness carrying the image forward, modified, interpreted, incorporated into different frameworks of meaning.

Hakim photographs the turtle with his phone, the digital image reducing three dimensions to two, colour to pixels, death to documentation. Why? The question arises after the action, the documentation preceding the purpose. Evidence? Memory? The photograph exists now in the phone's memory, will be uploaded to cloud storage, will persist in servers consuming electricity generated perhaps from natural gas extracted from beneath this very sea, the cycles of extraction and consumption so complex that causation becomes untraceable, responsibility diffuse, everything connected but nothing accountable.

The turtle's death is not a metaphor but a fact. Its species' decline is not symbolic but a measurable population collapse. The plastic in its throat is not human malice but systemic indifference, the externalities of convenience aggregating into extinction. Yet consciousness cannot encounter death without making meaning, cannot witness the ending without seeking pattern. The turtle becomes Mediterranean's condition made visible—

ancient species succumbing to contemporary chemistry, evolution outpaced by industrial transformation, deep time intersecting with accelerated time at this point on this beach where this child asks why and this mother responds with necessary fiction while truth decomposes in sunlight.

The walk continues, must continue, movement being consciousness's mode of processing, integration through ambulation. The sun approaches zenith, shadows contracting toward vanishing point, the day pivoting from morning to afternoon, though the transition is conceptual, imposed, the sun's movement being continuous, our categorization being convenience.

Returning toward the apartment but not yet ready for enclosure, Hakim finds another café, this one elevated, offering harbour view, tourist prices, the location's value extracted through economic rent. He orders water, not coffee, as hydration becomes necessary as the temperature exceeds the body's baseline. The water arrives in a plastic bottle—a company that claims water rights globally, that commodifies what was common, that profits from the enclosure of necessity. He drinks despite or through the contradiction, participation requiring compromise, purity being impossible, complicity being the condition of contemporary existence.

From this elevation, the harbour reveals its organization—zones of activity, patterns of movement, the syntax of maritime commerce. Fishing boats occupy the eastern section, their scale human, comprehensible. Cargo ships dominate the western section, their scale exceeding human proportion, sublime in the technical sense—awareness of magnitude that consciousness cannot fully accommodate. Between them, yachts cluster, the leisure class's vessels, mobility as luxury, the sea as playground rather than workplace.

The young scientist's words return: evolution in real-time. Not just bacterial but cultural, economic, and ecological. The harbour evolving from an ancient trade center to a modern industrial port to future uncertainty—climate change raising sea levels, temperature, acidity, the conditions that enabled this city's existence shifting beyond historical parameters. Alexandria, like all coastal cities, faces submersion, not immediately but inevitably, the ice sheets' stored water returning to liquid, seeking level, reclaiming what was always borrowed, temporarily emerged, the land's appearance above water being an exception, not a rule, in Earth's biography.

> Morning concludes, though morning never
> concludes, somewhere dawn is breaking as here
> noon approaches, the planet's rotation
> ensuring continuity, ensuring change, ensuring
> that no moment persists, that every

configuration is temporary. I have walked perhaps eight kilometres, have encountered perhaps a hundred people, and have exchanged words with some. The morning has taught what morning teaches: that the city continues, that knowledge circulates, that evolution proceeds indifferent to evaluation, that processes include us temporarily, that participation is not optional but only more or less conscious, more or less intentional. The harbour's polluted water will continue receiving swimmers, boats, and drainage. The library will continue asserting continuity. The turtle will be removed, but others will die, wash ashore, will be witnessed, and will become a story. None of this matters. All of this matters. Both statements true, neither complete, the paradox being not logical failure but accurate description of consciousness encountering world, making meaning from processes that exceed meaning, that preceded consciousness, that will continue when the last synapse fires its final signal, when the last book closes, when the last swimmer emerges from the sea that doesn't notice, doesn't care, doesn't stop.

The notebook closes. The pen returns to the pocket. The water bottle, emptied, remains on the table, its plastic persisting for centuries, breaking into smaller pieces but never disappearing, becoming microplastic that fish consume, that enters food chains, that circulates through bodies like the teacher's, like the child who asked about the turtle, the material trace of this moment's hydration spreading through space and time in patterns too complex to track but real nonetheless.

Time to return to the apartment to process what the morning has provided—encounters, recognitions, the city revealing itself through traversal, through participation, through the consciousness that walking enables, that sitting prevents, that makes the philosopher peripatetic by necessity, not choice.

# Noon

Noon: when shadows contract to nothing, when the sun occupies zenith, when Alexandria becomes what Durrell called "the white city," though white is absence, all wavelengths reflected, nothing absorbed, the city refusing light rather than accepting it.

Hakim, at another café, has chosen the table furthest from others, a corner position that enables observation while minimizing exposure—the anthropologist's location, the clinician's remove, though remove is fiction, consciousness always implicated in what it witnesses. The notebook lies open, pages bright enough to hurt, the pen's shadow the only mark until writing begins. Around him, the café's other occupants have arranged themselves according to social geometries he recognizes but doesn't enter: the businessmen conducting what business remains possible in Alexandria's economic constraints, the women whose leisure is performance, carefully constructed, the solitary man whose solitude differs from Hakim's—not chosen but imposed, isolation rather than withdrawal.

The waiter brings water without being asked—noon demands hydration, the body's water content requiring constant replenishment as perspiration attempts thermal regulation. The glass sweats immediately, condensation forming as water vapour meets surface cooled below the dew point, phase transition made visible. Hakim drinks, replaces loss, maintains the hydrochemical balance that enables consciousness, that seven-tenths water composition that makes humans marine organisms temporarily terrestrialized, carrying ocean within, salt concentration in blood matching ancient seas, evolution's memory written in sodium chloride.

> Alexandria: founded by Alexander, who came from Macedonia to conquer Egypt, who died in Babylon at thirty-two, whose body was brought here, displayed in a gold sarcophagus, then a glass one, then lost. The city begins in conquest, a foreign imposition that becomes native through duration, through forgetting. Ptolemaic dynasty: Greek pharaohs ruling Egypt for three centuries, Cleopatra the last, her suicide, Rome's victory, Augustus making Egypt personal property, bread basket, the Nile's fertility feeding the empire. Then Byzantium, a brief Persian interlude, the Arab conquest that brings Islam, that makes Egypt Arabic, though Egypt was never Arab before, becomes Arab through linguistic conversion, religious transformation, cultural conquest that calls itself liberation.

The pen moves across paper, thought becoming mark, mark becoming memory external to biological substrate, the notebook as prosthetic consciousness, extending mind beyond skull's boundaries.

Napoleon arrived in 1798, bringing scientists, linguists, and the Description de l'Égypte, which made Egypt an object of European knowledge, possession through documentation. Then Muhammad Ali, an Albanian mercenary who became Ottoman viceroy, became an autonomous ruler, a modernizer whose modernization means debt, means European capital penetrating the Egyptian economy. The British bombardment of 1882, the protectorate that protects British interests, and the Suez Canal as the jugular vein of the empire. Independence that isn't, a monarchy that serves foreign capital, revolution 1952, Nasser's Arab socialism that builds the High Dam, that nationalizes the canal, that makes Egypt the center of Arab consciousness briefly, before defeat, before Sadat's reversal, before the present.

Each conquest presents itself as liberation.

Alexander liberates from Persian rule. Rome liberates from Ptolemaic decay. Arabs liberate from Byzantine oppression. Napoleon liberates from Mamluk stagnation. British liberate from Oriental despotism. Nasser liberates from colonial subjugation. Each liberation becomes a new form of constraint. The pattern doesn't progress—it repeats with variations, like musical theme transposed through different keys, same structure, different tonal center.

The writing pauses. Through the café's shade, the noon sun creates a sharp boundary, bisecting the floor, dividing space into habitable and uninhabitable zones. A cat sleeps exactly at the boundary, half in shade, half in sun, the body's thermoregulation more sophisticated than conscious calculation, finding precisely the thermal equilibrium that enables maximum rest with minimum effort.

Two tourists enter, their skin already reddening from morning exposure, melanin insufficient for this latitude's ultraviolet intensity. They photograph themselves with a sea backdrop, discuss in loud voices their itinerary—the catacombs this afternoon, Pompey's Pillar tomorrow, the standard circuit that reduces Alexandria to its monuments, its dead history, missing the living city that continues despite or through tourism's extractive attention. They see Hakim writing, assume he's local, and ask in broken English for restaurant recommendations. He responds minimally, returns to the notebook before the conversation can establish itself.

Process philosophy accommodates benign processes too easily—growth, development, creative advance. But processes include degradation, exploitation, and forced participation. The slave trade was a process—human bodies circulated through the Atlantic system, transformed from persons to property to profit. Colonialism was a process—resources extracted, value transferred, metropolitan centers enriched through peripheral impoverishment. These processes created patterns that persist. Alexandria's wealth came from controlling trade between Europe and Asia, extracting rent from its geographic position. The wealth concentrated, displayed in palaces now submerged, while the peasants continued their seasonal cycles, their surplus appropriated by whatever dynasty claimed ownership.

Cancer is a process—cells proliferating without

constraint, circulation becoming metastasis, growth becoming pathology. In leukemia, blood cells forget their differentiation, return to a primitive state, multiply without purpose, and crowd out functional cells. The process continues until it doesn't, until chemotherapy's violence interrupts, or until the organism fails. Not all processes deserve continuation. Some require interruption, cessation, the difficult decision to stop what has begun, to refuse participation.

A family arrives at a nearby table—parents, two children, the domestic geometry that reproduces itself across cultures with variations in configuration but consistent in function. The children are perhaps eight and ten, the age where boredom is voiced rather than endured. They want to swim, to move, to be elsewhere. The parents want rest, shade, the pause that child-rearing rarely permits. The negotiation proceeds in Arabic fast enough that Hakim catches only fragments—promises, threats, the eventual compromise that satisfies no one but enables continuation.

The mother notices Hakim watching, offers an apologetic smile, the international gesture of parental exhaustion. He responds with a slight nod, acknowledgment without engagement, the interaction complete in its brevity. She returns to managing her children's energy, their bodies that reject stillness, that demand activity, that haven't yet learned capitalism's discipline of sitting, waiting, enduring.

The sea witnesses but doesn't judge. It received Phoenician traders and Roman galleys with equal indifference. It carried slaves from Africa and grain to Rome, the commercial traffic that makes atrocity routine. During the Second World War, it became a battlefield—Rommel and Montgomery, Afrika Korps and Desert Rats, the Mediterranean campaign that determined whether fascism or liberal democracy would control these waters, though for the colonized, the distinction was minimal, both systems extracting, both maintaining hierarchy through violence monopolized by the state.

Now it receives refugees—displaced seeking Europe's promise, finding often the sea's depth instead. The drownings number in thousands annually, bodies unrecovered, unmarked, the Mediterranean becomes a cemetery, an archive of attempted crossing. The boats are overloaded, engines insufficient, navigation by phone until batteries die, then stars, then hope, then nothing. Frontex patrols with thermal cameras, satellites track movement, the sea is surveilled·but not secured, and the processes of displacement continue despite or because of intervention.

The pen stops. The hand cramps from sustained writing, muscles fatigued, tendons inflamed. Hakim flexes fingers, rotates wrist, the small movements that restore circulation, that prevent repetitive stress injury, the occupational hazard of thought made material through inscription. The notebook remains open, the words visible but increasingly difficult to read in the sun's harsh light, the contrast between white paper and black ink diminishing as pupils contract, as eyes strain to maintain focus.

The waiter brings coffee, though Hakim didn't order it, the assumption that noon coffee is necessary is ritual, is what consciousness requires to persist through the day's heat. The small cup arrives with a glass of water, the pairing essential, caffeine's dehydration countered by parallel hydration, the body's chemistry maintained in an acceptable range through simultaneous opposing inputs.

Violence is not a deviation from process—it is

process, one among many, neither exceptional nor necessary, simply possible, often actual. The scorpion stings because its evolution equipped it with venom, not from malice but from process, pattern, the successful strategy reproduced. Humans developed the capacity for organized violence—weapons, armies, and the transformation of technology into force projection. This too is a process, neither good nor evil, categories that consciousness imposes but that processes don't recognize.

The ethical question is not whether to participate; participation is a given, involuntary condition of existence. The question is how to participate, with what degree of consciousness, toward what ends if ends exist, which process philosophy questions, denying teleology while unable to escape it entirely, consciousness being apparently purposive even if purpose is projection, interpretation, the meaning-making that distinguishes awareness from mere process.

Through the café's opening, the harbour is visible in partial view, the angle revealing a commercial dock where containers accumulate, their colours—red, blue, green—the only variation in industrial monotony. Each container is a standardized unit, twenty or forty feet, the dimensions that rationalize global trade, that make all ports equivalent, interchangeable, the specificities of place erased by logistics' requirements. Alexandria's harbour could be Rotterdam, Singapore, Los Angeles—the same cranes, same containers, same conversion of geography into a network node.

A ship is being unloaded, or loaded—from this distance, the direction of flow is invisible. The crane moves with mechanical precision, each container taking perhaps few minutes from ship to shore or shore to ship, the rhythm hypnotic, industrial process at its most refined, human labor minimized, mostly eliminated, the dock workers who once made ports centers of radical politics replaced by operators in air-conditioned cabins, pushing buttons, moving joysticks, their bodies protected from heat, from weather, from the material reality of what they move.

> Capital accumulates through circulation, Marx observed, though observed is wrong—he diagnosed, analyzed, performed conceptual surgery on capitalism's logic. The commodity must move to realize value, must transform from product to money to product again, the

cycle accelerating with each technical innovation. Containerization was such an innovation—reducing loading time from days to hours, eliminating theft, and standardizing handling. The sea adapted, ports dredged deeper, ships enlarged, economies of scale pursued until ships became too large.

The Mediterranean is marginal now in global shipping—neither Pacific nor Atlantic volume, neither Chinese production nor American consumption at a sufficient scale. It serves regional trade, tourism, the movement of people deemed illegal, weapons deemed necessary, and drugs deemed profitable despite or because of prohibition. The sea that was once the center is now the periphery, though center and periphery are relative, positional; the view from Alexandria is different from that from Brussels, from Damascus, from Tripoli.

The tourists have left, payment left on the table, tip insufficient by local standards, but they don't know, won't learn, will repeat the error at each establishment, their ignorance protected by economic asymmetry, their euros worth enough that precision doesn't matter. The waiter clears their table without expression, the tip disappearing into a pocket, the accumulation of small amounts that might, aggregated, enable something—rent payment, medical procedure, child's education, the investments in future that poverty makes difficult, sometimes impossible.

The family continues their negotiation, the children's energy temporarily contained by phones, screens pacifying what parental authority couldn't, the devices that transform children into consumers of content, attention harvested, data extracted, behavioural patterns analyzed, predicted, modified through algorithmic intervention. The parents, too, consult phones, the family together but separate, each consciousness interfacing with a different network, different flow of information, the table they share merely physical proximity, not social unity.

> The heat is fact, not metaphor. Thirty-seven degrees Celsius in shade, higher in the sun, humidity from the sea making evaporative cooling inefficient. The body responds— vasodilation, perspiration, behavioural adaptation (seeking shade, reducing movement). But sustained heat stress degrades cognitive function, increases irritability, correlates with violence, the summer murder

rate exceeding winter's, the temperature's effect on consciousness is measurable, predictable, and ignored in discussions of political violence that prefer ideological explanation to thermodynamic.

Climate change will make Alexandria uninhabitable, not immediately but within a century, probably sooner. A sea level rise of two meters, the conservative projection, submerges the Corniche, the harbour. But before submersion, heat—wet bulb temperatures exceeding thirty-five degrees, the threshold beyond which human bodies cannot cool themselves, when perspiration fails, when shade provides no relief, when even rest becomes lethal. The wealthy will migrate, have already begun, to their properties in cooler latitudes, their mobility purchased. The poor will remain, will adapt until adaptation fails, will die in place, their deaths statistics in reports that recommend mitigation, adaptation, resilience, the language that admits defeat without acknowledging responsibility.

Hakim closes the notebook, the writing becoming

forced, the thoughts too dark for noon's harsh light, though darkness and light are not opposed but complementary, the full spectrum necessary for vision, for comprehension, for the honest account that participatory philosophy demands if it's to be more than academic exercise, more than comfortable abstraction that avoids violence, suffering, the processes that consciousness wishes weren't but are.

Standing brings vertigo, brief but concerning—the heat's effect, dehydration despite water consumed, the body announcing its limits, its objection to conditions that consciousness chose but that cellular processes didn't, couldn't, evolution not anticipating air conditioning's absence, the body expecting technological mediation that isn't available, not here, not now.

The walk to the apartment will be brief but difficult, the sun at zenith making every surface radiate, the city becomes a furnace, the air itself seemingly solid, resistant, requiring effort to traverse. But traverse he must, the alternative being continued sitting, continued exposure, the heat accumulating in the body until systems fail, until consciousness retreats, until the processes that enable awareness cease their coordination.

> The Mediterranean doesn't care. This phrase recurs because it's true. After all, consciousness projects care onto a world that doesn't reciprocate, that continues its processes

indifferent to meaning, to suffering, to the beauty and horror consciousness discovers, creates, and endures. The sea will outlast Alexandria, will outlast humanity, will continue until Earth's water evaporates as the sun expands, becomes a red giant, makes this planet what Venus is now—greenhouse beyond life's tolerance, the processes of chemistry continuing without biology, without consciousness, without witness.

But consciousness does care, can't not care, the meaning-making compulsion that might be error, might be gift, might be simply what this configuration of matter does under these conditions, for this duration, until it doesn't. To care without reciprocation, to make meaning in a meaningless universe, to continue despite futility—this too is process, perhaps the most difficult, certainly the most human, possibly the most temporary.

He walks toward the apartment, the street's heat shimmer making the buildings appear to undulate, solid become liquid, the phase transition that heat suggests but doesn't actually accomplish, the buildings remaining solid despite appearance, the permanence that is not permanent but persistent enough for human purposes, for the fiction of stability that civilization requires, that consciousness assumes despite knowing better.

The sea remains visible peripherally, its noon blue now white with glare, painful to perceive directly, the Mediterranean at its least accommodating, its least romantic, its most honest—not the wine-dark sea of poetry but the bright burning surface that reflects rather than absorbs, that makes vision painful, that reminds consciousness of its limits, its vulnerability, its temporary permission to witness processes that preceded it, that continue through it, that will persist beyond it.

A door opens—shade, stairs, ascent to apartment that waits, that provides shelter, that enables continuation through afternoon's heat toward evening's promise of cooling, of softening light, of the day's arc continuing toward conclusion that is not conclusion but transition, darkness returning, the cycle continuing, the process that includes this consciousness today, temporarily, gratefully, despite everything, because of everything.

The apartment door closes behind him. The heat remains outside, mostly. The shutters remain closed, maintaining darkness that is cooler than light, the simple physics of radiation and absorption, the strategies that predate air conditioning, that make life possible at this latitude, this season, this moment in the anthropocene that is ending the holocene, that is creating new processes, new patterns, new forms of suffering and possibly, not certainly, new forms of consciousness adequate to what comes next, what is already arriving, what cannot be stopped only witnessed, endured, possibly survived.

He drinks water, sits, opens the notebook again, and reads what was written in the café's harsh light. The words remain, the thoughts fixed in ink, the morning's meditation on power, violence, the dark processes that participatory philosophy must acknowledge if it is to be honest, if it is to be more than consolation, more than evasion, more than the academic exercise that makes suffering abstract, manageable, publishable.

> Noon teaches what noon teaches: that maximum illumination creates maximum shadow, that seeing everything means seeing nothing, that the body has limits consciousness ignores at its peril, that the sea continues indifferent to witness, that processes include violence as surely as they include growth, that participation is not always voluntary, that some processes require interruption, that others continue despite our wish they wouldn't, that consciousness makes meaning from meaninglessness, that this might be error or gift or simply what happens when matter organizes at this level of complexity, for this

duration, in this place, at this time, under this sun that burns without malice, that gives life and death with equal indifference, that makes possible the very consciousness that questions it, that will outlast the questions, the questioner, the questioned, everything except the process itself, which has no name, needs no name, continues without naming.

The pen stops. The notebook closes. Noon passes into afternoon, the sun beginning its descent from zenith.

## AFTERNOON

Two o'clock and the heat has achieved what physicists call steady state—maximum sustained intensity without further increase, the sun's angle beginning its decline from zenith, but radiation accumulated in stone, in asphalt, in the city's material substrate continuing to emit, the urban heat island effect.

Hakim emerges from the apartment into heat that has weight, presence, almost personality—malevolent but not personal, the malevolence of physics, of thermodynamics pursuing equilibrium through consciousness's discomfort. The body adapts, must adapt, vasodilation increasing, pulse quickening to maintain circulation despite blood vessels' expansion, the cardiovascular system working harder to achieve what cool air enables without effort.

Each step requires decision, commitment, the will to continue despite cellular objection, despite evolutionary programming that says seek shade, reduce activity, wait for evening's cooling that will come, must come, has always come, though always is brief in geological time, climate being variable across scales consciousness barely comprehends.

West again, but further than morning's circuit. The streets narrow as he moves inland from the Corniche, away from tourist Alexandria, from cosmopolitan pretensions, toward the Alexandria he'd imagined from reading Durrell's city, Cavafy's, the philosophical capital that existed more in text than territory.

Hakim walked into the Alexandria that Alexandrians inhabit when not performing for a foreign gaze. Laundry hangs between buildings, a semaphore of domestic life, clothes drying in heat that evaporates water faster than sun bleaches colour. Children play football in an alley, the ball improvised from plastic bags wrapped with string, the goal marked by sandals, the game proceeding according to rules both universal and local, disputes resolved through volume rather than authority.

He passes a mosque, not historic, not notable, one of thousands that punctuate the city, that make sacred space from ordinary architecture. The afternoon call to prayer has passed, or has not yet arrived, temporal orientation becoming uncertain in the heat that makes duration elastic. Through an open doorway, darkness that promises coolness, men arranging themselves on carpets, the geometric precision of prayer that makes community from individual bodies, that synchronizes consciousness through synchronized posture.

The notebook remains in the apartment, but consciousness continues its inscription, thought proceeding through internal dialogue, the self split into observer and observed, the doubling that enables reflection but prevents presence, always already removed from immediate experience by the gap that consciousness is, or creates, or suffers.

A building presents itself—the balconies' pattern, their wrought iron baroque, despite the building's otherwise minimal ornamentation. An old man sits in the doorway's shade, watching without seeming to watch, the surveillance that the elderly perform in neighbourhoods worldwide, the informal security that knows who belongs, who doesn't, who might be. Hakim approaches, Arabic rusty but functional, asks about the building's history, carefully indirect, the circumlocution that politeness requires.

They discuss the neighbourhood's changes—the new shopping center that displaced the informal market, the school that closed, then reopened as a language institute, the mosque that expanded, consuming adjacent buildings. The man has witnessed it all, recorded nothing, his memory the only archive, unreliable, precious, disappearing with each death, each departure.

"The sea doesn't change," the man says eventually, perhaps a conversational formula, perhaps a deeper recognition that while human constructions transform, the Mediterranean persists, its cycles longer than human generations, its memory written in currents, temperatures, chemistry rather than consciousness.

Hakim continues walking, fewer shops, more life lived rather than commercialized. Women talk between doorways, their conversation pausing as he passes, resuming with slight modulation, his presence noted, incorporated, accommodated without welcome or rejection, the neutrality that urban density requires, enables, enforces. Children everywhere—school being out, or not in session, or truancy tolerated in the heat that makes learning impossible. They play games whose rules emerge from play itself, disputes arising, resolving, arising again, and the social learning that precedes formal education, which might be more essential.

The afternoon continues its arc toward evening, the sun lowering, the shadows beginning to lengthen though still harsh, still sharp, the light that reveals texture, detail, the accumulated damage that surfaces bear—weather, use, time's passage written in material degradation. He walks without destination now, the search abandoned or fulfilled through abandonment, each street equally meaningful or meaningless, the city revealing itself as present reality, what exists now, what continues despite or through transformation.

A sound draws attention—splashing, laughter, the acoustic signature of water play. Following it leads to a small square where children swim in a fountain not designed for swimming, their bodies adapting the space to their needs, the official purpose subverted, superseded. They jump from the fountain's edge, perhaps meter high, the water perhaps meter deep, the danger minimal but real, the risk that makes play meaningful, that distinguishes it from entertainment, from the supervised safety that privilege provides, demands.

The children are of various ages, maybe six to twelve, the older ones monitoring the younger without seeming to, the informal care that communities provide when formal structures fail or never existed. Their joy is uncomplicated, or seems so from the outside, from an adult perspective that reads joy where it might be simple cooling, simple occupation of time that must be occupied somehow.

One boy, perhaps ten, executes a backwards flip, the motion practiced, perfected, performed for applause that comes from his peers, from watching adults, from the city that needs joy, that takes it where found. He climbs out, prepares to repeat, notices Hakim watching, performs again with slight exaggeration, the showing off that childhood permits, requires, the establishment of identity through demonstrated capability.

An old man sits on a bench near the fountain, watching the children with an expression that might be simple attendance without evaluation. Hakim sits at the bench's other end, the distance calibrated—close enough for potential conversation, far enough to avoid obligation. They watch together, the children's energy seemingly infinite though finite, obviously, entropy applies to play as to all processes.

"Every afternoon," the man says eventually, Arabic slow, clear, accommodating Hakim's foreign presence without acknowledging it.

"The same children?"

"Some same, some different. The fountain is constant."

The fountain is constant. The phrase carries weight beyond its simplicity—the fixed point around which variation orbits, the stability that enables change, the stage that remains while actors transform.

"You have grandchildren among them?"

"No. My children left. Germany, two. America, one. They have children I've seen only in photographs. Digital. The phone shows me grandchildren I'll never touch."

The statement is matter-of-fact, loss presented without sentiment, the global dispersion of families that modernity enables, requires, and normalizes. The man's children succeeded, escaped, abandoned—all terms accurate, none complete.

"You stayed."

"Someone must stay. The city requires witnesses. Otherwise, it's just buildings. The children—" he gestures toward the fountain, "—they don't know they're keeping Alexandria alive. They think they're just swimming. But without them, what is the city? Museums? Hotels? The stones the tourists photograph? The city is this—children in fountains, illegally, temporarily, necessarily."

The city requires witnesses. The phrase articulates something essential about place, about duration, about the difference between space and place. Space is coordinates, geometry, the abstract grid that mapping imposes. Place is lived, witnessed, the accumulation of moments that consciousness attends to, that memory preserves however inaccurately, that creates meaning from mere matter. Alexandria has been witnessed for two millennia, continuously if not consistently, the witnesses changing but witnessing continuing, the city persisting through being perceived, through participating in consciousness that participates in it.

The children tire, finally, their energy depleted or redirected. They disperse, the fountain returning to its official function—decoration, civic beautification, the water circulating without purpose beyond circulation itself. The old man walks away without goodbye, the interaction complete, its wisdom delivered or received or both or neither, the words continuing to resonate as Hakim remains seated, watching the empty fountain, the water that continues its circulation, its process, indifferent to observation.

The light is changing rapidly now, the sun perhaps an hour from the horizon, the shadows long, the heat beginning its barely perceptible decrease. Time to walk again, to move toward evening, toward the day's next phase, the continuation that is not repetition but variation, the same structure with different content, the pattern that persists through transformation.

Hakim rises and walks toward the Corniche, which appears with the sea beyond it gold now, the sun low enough that looking is possible though still difficult, the glare decreased but not eliminated. He could continue to the apartment, could rest before evening's walk, but momentum carries him forward, toward the sea that has been the destination, the background, the constant through the day's variations.

At the sea wall, different from morning's position, different light revealing different surface, he stops, watches, the simple attention that asks nothing, expects nothing, receives what is given—waves, light, the intersection of fluid and electromagnetic radiation that creates what we call beauty though beauty is category imposed, not inherent, the sea being neither beautiful nor ugly but simply what it is, process continuing, pattern persisting. The Mediterranean that has been here, will be here, until it isn't, until conditions change beyond the parameters that allow liquid water, that permit seas, that enable consciousness to perceive, to name, to assign meaning that the sea neither acknowledges nor refuses, simply continues through, despite, because of, the categories becoming irrelevant against the fact of water moving, always moving, the circulation that defines sea as different from lake, from pond, from the contained water that stagnates, that dies, while the sea continues, connects, circulates, the process that includes everything, excludes nothing, continues regardless.

# EVENING

Six o'clock and the sun has begun its calculated descent. The Corniche has become a theatre, a stage for evening's performance, the daily gathering that makes public space social space, that transforms geography into community, temporarily, provisionally.

Hakim walks westward now, the sea to his right has begun its chromatic sequence—the blue deepening, complexifying, becoming what language fails to specify: blue with undertones of green where depth increases, purple where angle permits, gold where sun strikes directly, the color not stable but processual, each wave face presenting different surface, different reflection, different participation in light's interaction with matter.

The crowd has materialized as if from nowhere, though from everywhere actually—apartments releasing their inhabitants as heat decreases, shops closing or opening depending on commercial logic, the city's population redistributing itself from interior to exterior, from private to public, the circulation that evening enables, requires, and celebrates. Families walk in formations that declare relationships—parents flanking children, grandparents following slowly, the generations synchronized temporarily despite different velocities, different destinations, different relationships to time's passage.

A young couple passes, her hand touching his arm briefly, the contact minimal but significant, the public display of affection that Alexandria permits within strict parameters, the negotiation between desire and propriety that every culture manages differently, that here requires subtlety, coding, the messages transmitted through gesture rather than declaration. They walk close but not too close, together but maintaining plausible deniability, the relationship existing in liminal space between the sanctioned and the forbidden, the zone where most life actually occurs.

The evening promenade—la passeggiata in Italian, el paseo in Spanish, but no specific Arabic term, the practice transcending linguistic boundaries, occurring wherever humans concentrate along coasts, the sea drawing consciousness toward itself as gravity draws mass, or as mass creates gravity, the causation ambiguous, bidirectional. Every Mediterranean city performs this ritual, has performed it for centuries, will continue until cities cease or seas dry or humans evolve beyond the need for collective presence, for the confirmation that others exist, that solitude is chosen rather than imposed, that the day ends with witness, with participation in something larger than individual consciousness but smaller than abstract humanity.

Vendors have established positions along the wall— corn grilled over charcoal, the smoke carrying caramelized sweetness; nuts measured in paper cones, salt crystallizing on warm surfaces; tea in glasses that burn fingers, requiring careful handling, the minor risk that makes consumption intentional rather than automatic. The economics of it: small amounts, small prices, the accumulation that might enable survival but not prosperity, the informal sector that employs thousands, that exists outside taxation, regulation, the official economy that pretends to encompass all exchange but captures only what chooses visibility.

Music arrives—an oud player, perhaps sixty, the instrument worn but maintained, the wood polished by decades of handling. He plays without amplification, the sound barely audible above conversation, traffic, the sea's constant presence, but audible enough for those who choose to listen, who pause in their walking, who recognize in the melody something older than the city. A few coins accumulate in the case, enough for tea, for bread, for another evening's performance, the cycle continuing.

Children run between walkers, their energy inexhaustible, apparently, though exhaustion will come, suddenly, completely, the collapse that parents anticipate, prepare for, the carrying home of sleeping bodies that moments before were perpetual motion. They chase pigeons that barely flee, that have adapted to human density, that continue their scavenging undisturbed by anything short of direct contact. The birds, too, are part of the evening's ecology, their presence neither welcomed nor prevented, simply accepted as a consequence of human concentration, of food dropped, discarded, the waste that becomes a resource in a different metabolic cycle.

"The sea is generous today."

The voice is familiar—the fisherman from dawn, now returning or still here or here again, the temporal sequence uncertain. He carries no fish, no equipment, the evidence of his profession absent, but the weathering remains, the skin that declares decades of solar exposure, salt accumulation, the body marked by its environment, shaped by repetitive action, the shoulders that have pulled nets, the hands that have gutted fish, the knowledge embodied rather than abstracted.

"The city requires witnessing."

The phrase emerges without planning, the echo of afternoon's old man, the wisdom borrowed, transmitted, modified in transmission. The fisherman nods, understanding or seeming to, the acceptance that doesn't require elaboration.

"Tomorrow I fish before dawn. Same time, same place. The sea doesn't wait, but it doesn't hurry."

He moves on, the interaction complete, its brevity sufficient, the exchange of recognition that doesn't become obligation, that acknowledges shared presence without demanding continued engagement. This too is urban knowledge—when to engage, when to release, the calibration of social distance that makes density bearable.

> The sea doesn't wait, but it doesn't hurry. The temporal paradox that contains truth: processes proceed at their own rates, neither accelerated by desire nor delayed by reluctance. The tide rises and falls according to lunar gravity, not human need. Fish migrate following temperature gradients, food sources, and reproductive imperatives that consciousness can map but not modify. The fisherman knows this, works within it rather than against it, the submission to patterns larger than the individual will that makes his profession possible, that makes any engagement with nature more than extraction, that becomes participation, collaboration, the mutual modification that doesn't require mutual recognition.

The sun has descended to perhaps twenty degrees above the horizon, the angle that photographers pursue, that makes surfaces gold, that transforms the ordinary through illumination that won't last, that is precious because it is temporary.

The crowd has thickened, the Corniche now dense with bodies, the flow resembling fluid dynamics, laminar where space permits, turbulent at obstacles, eddies forming behind vendors, around musicians, the physics of crowds that mirrors the physics of fluids, same equations, different scales.

A young girl takes a selfie with sunset behind her, the image reviewed, deleted, retaken, the iteration continuing until satisfaction or exhaustion, the documentation that precedes experience, that might replace experience, the photograph more real than the moment it claims to preserve. Her friend watches, waits, and offers to take a photo that includes both—the paradox of staged authenticity that social media demands, rewards, and normalizes.

Beyond them, the sun touches a cloud layer that hasn't been visible until now, the moisture invisible until light reveals it, transforms it, and makes it spectacular, temporarily. The colours proliferate—orange, pink, purple, the spectrum's warm end dominating while blue retreats, persists only in zenith, the sky becomes a gradient, transition made visible. The crowd notices, some stopping to observe, others continuing their walk, the sunset ordinary through repetition, through reliability, the spectacle that happens daily therefore barely happens, consciousness habituating to wonder, requiring novelty that nature doesn't provide, proceeding through cycles that vary within patterns, that repeat without exact repetition.

> Beauty is consciousness's category, not nature's. The sunset proceeds according to physics—Rayleigh scattering, atmospheric refraction, and the geometry of celestial mechanics. The colours exist in perception, wavelengths interpreted by neural processing that evolved for different purposes, that find beauty where utility once existed, the aesthetic judgment that might be an evolutionary spandrel, an accidental consequence of pattern recognition necessary for survival. But knowing the physics doesn't diminish the experience, might enhance it—*understanding process while participating in it*, the double consciousness that science enables, that poetry preceded, that philosophy attempts to reconcile.

He finds a space at the wall, claims it through presence, the informal property rights that govern public space, which last only while occupied, and that dissolve with departure. The stone is warm still from day's accumulation, the thermal mass releasing slowly what it absorbed quickly, the hysteresis that makes coastal climates moderate, that makes the Mediterranean's shores habitable, that will make them uninhabitable when temperatures exceed what the stone can buffer, what bodies can endure.

An old man stands nearby, perhaps the same from the afternoon's fountain, perhaps different, the elderly becoming a category rather than individuals in consciousness that doesn't attend carefully, that generalizes from limited samples, that sees pattern where there might be randomness. He watches the sunset with attention that suggests practice, routine, the daily observation that might be meditation, might be a simple occupation of time that must be occupied somehow, that stretches when productivity ceases, when purpose becomes survival rather than accomplishment.

"Every evening?" Hakim asks the question that is also acknowledgment, invitation, and the opening of potential exchange.

"When possible. Which is usually. At my age, everything is usually or never."

The response carries humour without joke, the acceptance of the constraint that age imposes, that consciousness recognizes but the body experiences, the difference between knowing and being that philosophy articulates but life demonstrates.

"You're not from here," the man continues. "I thought I would find something," Hakim offers, the admission incomplete but sufficient.

"You came to discover you can't arrive at what was only textual, but you found what everyone finds—difference. But difference from what?

The man's Arabic is formal, educated, the syntax of someone who reads, who thinks in structured ways, who might have been a teacher, scholar, one of Alexandria's intellectuals who stayed when others left, who maintained civilization's conversation in place while others carried it elsewhere.

"You taught," Hakim suggests, reading the signs, the posture, the particular attention to language's precision.

"Philosophy. At the University. Forty years. Retired now, which means I do the same thing without office, without students, without purpose except purpose itself. I read, I think, I watch sunset, I sleep, I wake, I continue. Same activity, different audience. Or no audience, which might be more honest. Philosophy performed for witnesses becomes performance, loses something essential. Philosophy without an audience might be madness, but it might be purity. The distinction is unclear and might be meaningless. The examined life, which Socrates said was the only life worth living, though he didn't live long enough to test the hypothesis fully."

> Philosophy without an audience might be madness, but it might be purity. This is the question that haunts all thinking that thinks

about thinking—is consciousness examining itself productive or recursive, does it generate insight or infinite regress, does it approach truth or create elaborate fictions that console but don't correspond. The examined life might be worth living, but is examining the examined life worth doing, and examining that examination, the recursion that philosophy enables, suffers, might be its glory or might be its failure.

They stand together, watching the sun approach the horizon, the disc now visible without pain, the intensity diminished enough that looking is possible, that the eye can perceive the sphere that is always there but usually unbearable, the source that makes sight possible but blinds when observed directly, the paradox of illumination that reveals everything except itself.

*"The sea does not care,"* the philosopher says, "which is why it's perfect. Every wave is new water arranged in an ancient pattern. Identity without substance, form without matter, or rather form constantly acquiring new matter, discarding it, acquiring again. This is what we are too—patterns temporarily organized, mistaking ourselves for permanent, discovering impermanence, struggling to accept what was always obvious."

Every wave is new water arranged in an ancient pattern. This is *process philosophy* articulated simply, precisely, the wisdom that doesn't require technical terminology, that emerges from observation, from attention sustained over decades, from the thinking that walking enables, that sitting prevents, that makes philosophy peripatetic necessarily, not arbitrarily. The pattern persists while matter transforms—this is identity, this is consciousness, this is everything that seems stable but is actually dynamic equilibrium, the balance that requires constant adjustment, constant energy, constant participation.

The sun touches the horizon now, the moment that is not moment but duration, the disc's lower edge meeting the line that is not line but curve, the Earth's rotation made visible or rather the effect of rotation, the relative motion that consciousness experiences as sunset, though nothing sets, nothing rises, the language preserving pre-Copernican cosmology, the phenomenology that persists despite knowledge, that remains true experientially while false astronomically.

The crowd has quieted, not silent but subdued, the collective attention that sunset commands, that makes strangers a temporary community, witnessing together what each could witness alone but chooses not to, the gathering that makes an event from occurrence, that transforms daily process into ritual, into the repetition that creates culture, that distinguishes human consciousness from mere awareness.

Musicians have multiplied—the oud player joined by a tabla drummer, the rhythm establishing itself, finding the tempo that walking creates, that bodies recognize, that makes movement music and music movement. Some children dance, their movements unselfconscious, uncalculated, the response that precedes thought, that thought later inhibits, that adulthood mostly eliminates except in moments when consciousness relaxes its control, permits body its knowledge, its own intelligence that modernism calls primitive but is actually primary, foundational, the wisdom of muscle and bone that preceded language, that will outlast it.

The sun is half-disappeared now, the process accelerating apparently, though the rate is constant, the perception shifting as reference points change, as the disc's visible portion diminishes, as consciousness attends more carefully, knowing conclusion approaches. The colors have deepened—orange becoming red, purple darkening toward violet, the blue overhead persisting but different blue, darker, preparing for night's arrival that is not arrival but continuation, the spectrum shifting beyond visible, the infrared that bodies feel as warmth, the ultraviolet that damages but doesn't announce itself, the electromagnetic radiation that consciousness samples narrowly, interprets partially, mistakes for complete.

Sunset is not an event but a process, not a conclusion but a transition. The sun continues its fusion, the Earth continues its rotation, the only ending is in consciousness that divides continuous process into discrete moments, that creates boundaries where none exist, that makes meaning from patterns that proceed without meaning, that don't require meaning, that exist before meaning and will exist after. We are sunset's witnesses, not its purpose. It would proceed without us, has proceeded for billions of years without consciousness, will proceed after consciousness ceases, the universe continuing its expansion, its transformation toward heat death that is not death but a different configuration, different process, the possibility we can't imagine because imagination requires negentropy that won't exist, can't exist, in a universe at thermal equilibrium.

The philosopher has been quiet, watching, perhaps thinking or perhaps not, the attention that doesn't require thought, that might be thought's absence, the awareness without analysis that meditation seeks, that walking sometimes enables, that sunset might facilitate through beauty that overwhelms cognitive processing, that forces consciousness to receive rather than interpret, to participate rather than evaluate.

"You wrote today," he observes, noting something—ink stains perhaps, or the particular fatigue that sustained writing produces, or simply the deduction from Hakim's manner, the way consciousness shaped by writing carries itself, announces itself.

"Notes. Observations. Trying to understand something."

"Understanding is overvalued. Participating is undervalued. The sea doesn't understand itself, but continues. The sun doesn't understand fusion, but fuses. Understanding is consciousness's compensation for not being able to simply *be*, to continue without question, to process without purpose."

The statement could be nihilistic, but it isn't; it carries acceptance rather than resignation, the wisdom that comes from thinking through to thought's limits, discovering what lies beyond, which is not nothing but something else, something that doesn't require articulation, that exists without language, that language points toward but can't contain.

The sun's final edge disappears, the moment marked by some with photographs, by others with silence, by children with indifference, their games continuing, their energy not yet depleted. The sky continues its chromatic display, the colors persisting after their source has passed below horizon, the atmosphere itself luminous, scattering light that arrives indirectly, the sunset that continues after sunset, the process that doesn't conclude but transforms, continues elsewhere, the terminator sweeping westward, bringing night here, day there, the planet's rotation ensuring that every sunset is also sunrise, every ending also beginning, the cycle that is not cycle but spiral, repetition with variation, pattern with progress or at least change, which might be progress, might be decay, might be simply difference without evaluation.

"Walk with me," the philosopher suggests, beginning to move before response, assuming acceptance, the invitation that is barely an invitation, more observation that walking will occur, that consciousness at rest tends toward rest, while consciousness in motion tends toward motion, the inertia that applies to thought as to matter.

They walk eastward now, the sun behind them. The crowd has begun to thin slightly, families with young children departing, the demographic shifting toward adolescents, young adults, those whose evening extends beyond sunset, whose social life begins when families' end.

"You practice medicine," the philosopher observes, states, and knows somehow.

"Practiced. Blood," Hakim replied.

"The most philosophical of substances. Liquid but structured, identical but unique, constantly renewed but recognizably continuous. Blood is a process made visible, made vital. Without circulation, blood is just fluid. Without blood, circulation is just plumbing."

The observation is accurate, insightful, the connection between medical and philosophical that Hakim has thought but not articulated, which requires external confirmation, the recognition that thinking alone doesn't provide, that makes conversation necessary despite thought's tendency toward solitude.

They continue walking, the rhythm established, the pace that enables conversation without breathlessness, that synchronizes their movements, that creates temporary unity from separate consciousnesses, the shared ambulation that might be communication's oldest form, preceding language, the walking together that establishes trust, that enables exchange, that makes strangers into temporary companions.

The stars have begun to appear, not suddenly but gradually, the brightest first—Venus probably, though planets don't twinkle, the steady light that distinguishes them from stars whose light atmospheric turbulence disturbs, makes dance, the scintillation that poetry celebrates but astronomy corrects for, the distortion that must be subtracted to see clearly what distance and time have brought to visibility.

"Alexandria had astronomers," the philosopher notes,

following Hakim's gaze upward. "Mapped the stars, calculated orbits, and understood celestial mechanics centuries before telescopes. The Library wasn't just a storage but a laboratory, observatory, the place where knowledge was produced, not just preserved. We forget that, imagine it as an archive when it was actually a workshop, the place where understanding was manufactured, processed, refined."

"And lost," Hakim adds, the obvious conclusion.

"Lost implies it existed stably, could be preserved. But knowledge is a process, not a product. It exists only in transmission, in teaching, in the movement from mind to mind. The Library burned, yes, but the librarians dispersed, carried what they remembered, taught elsewhere, the diaspora that preserved through transformation what storage couldn't maintain unchanged."

> Knowledge is a process, not a product. This reformulation challenges everything academic culture assumes: the publications that fix thought in text, the libraries that store publications, the citations that create genealogies of ideas as if ideas were objects rather than events, things rather than happenings. But every reading is a new reading, every understanding is a new understanding,

the text might be stable, but interpretation isn't, can't be, the meaning emerging from interaction between consciousness and marks on page, the participation that makes dead letters living thought, temporarily, until attention moves elsewhere.

The Corniche continues, seems infinite though finite obviously, Alexandria's edge being defined, limited, where Mediterranean meets land, the boundaries that seem permanent but are negotiated constantly, the sea claiming land through erosion, storms, the land claiming sea through sedimentation, construction, the interface that is not line but zone, area of contest, exchange, the liminal space where categories blur.

"You visit but don't stay," the philosopher observes, predicts, and knows.

"Probably not. The visit was necessary but not sustainable. I came to..." Hakim pauses, the purpose suddenly unclear, inarticulate, the motivation that seemed obvious now mysterious, the forces that produced the visit too complex to name simply.

"You came to discover you can't stay. Everyone does. The emigrants, especially the successful ones, particularly. They achieve elsewhere what here was impossible, then discover achievement doesn't satisfy, that success is local, contextual, that what matters there doesn't matter here, that here doesn't exist anyway, has become there while you were away, the place transformed by your absence as much as by time's passage."

The diagnosis is accurate, uncomfortable, the truth that Hakim has been discovering all day made explicit, external, and undeniable. The philosopher continues:

"But the attempt matters. The walking, the witnessing, the writing you did today. Not because it discovers anything but because it processes, transforms, enables tomorrow's difference. You'll leave Alexandria but Alexandria won't leave you, will continue in memory that will continue lying, creating, making meaning from patterns that exceed meaning. This is participation—not presence but process, not being here but having been here, the past that enables future, the accumulation that makes consciousness more than immediate awareness."

They've reached a pause, a place where the philosopher apparently intends to stop, to turn, to continue alone or elsewhere. The interaction is concluding, has reached its natural term, the exchange is complete, though completion is always arbitrary, provisional, the conversation could continue, but won't, the timing that social intelligence recognizes, respects.

"Tomorrow morning," the philosopher says, "same sun, same sea, different consciousness observing. The repetition that is never repetition, the pattern that persists through variation, the process that includes us temporarily. Walk early, before the heat. Think less, observe more. Write if you must, but remember writing is also a process, also a transformation, the meaning you create is not discovered but made, manufactured, the product that is actually production, the making that never completes."

He walks away without farewell, the departure that doesn't require ceremony, the urban anonymity that permits encounter without obligation, exchange without commitment, the freedom that density enables, that makes cities laboratories for consciousness, for the experiments in living that suburbs prevent, that villages prohibit, that only the metropolitan allows, demands, and makes possible.

Hakim stands alone now, the evening continuing around him, through him, the crowd that has thinned but not disappeared, the energy that has shifted from familial to social, from display to encounter, the night beginning its different processes, its different possibilities.

The walk back is quick, directed, the body knowing the route now, the cognitive map established, the efficiency that familiarity enables. The streets are different at night—lit differently, populated differently, the same coordinates containing a different city, the nocturnal Alexandria that coexists with diurnal, that occupies the same space but different time, the temporal zoning that makes multiple cities possible in a single location.

The apartment building is quiet, the stairs dark, the ascent careful, touch supplementing vision, the proprioceptive knowledge that bodies develop, which makes navigation possible without sight, the backup systems that consciousness doesn't acknowledge until needed. The door opens to a space that is beginning to become familiar, the repetition that makes strange into known, that transforms space into place through duration, through return, through the accumulation of moments that memory will reconstruct, falsify, and make meaningful.

> Today is complete but not concluded, will continue in memory, in dream, in tomorrow's difference that today enables. The Mediterranean continues its circulation, its process, its indifference that is not hostility but freedom, the freedom from meaning that enables meaning, that makes consciousness possible, necessary, temporary, grateful.

The pen stops, the notebook closes, and evening yields to night.

# NIGHT

Eight-thirty and darkness has begun its establishment, not arrival but intensification, the photons decreasing exponentially, the electromagnetic radiation shifting beyond visible spectrum, the infrared that bodies emit, detect through thermal receptors, the heat signatures that make us visible to different sensors, the night vision that technology enables, that evolution provided to nocturnal predators but not to primates whose ancestors chose daylight, traded night vision for color discrimination, the evolutionary bargain that makes darkness foreign to consciousness that depends on light for more than sight, for the metaphors that structure thought itself—enlightenment, illumination, clarity, the cognitive dependence on optical experience.

The Corniche has transformed, demographically, energetically, the families replaced by different congregations—young men in groups whose solidarity is performed through proximity, volume, the occupation of space that asserts presence, claims territory, establishes identity through collective embodiment. Young women are also in groups, but differently configured; the protection that numbers provide, the surveillance that continues despite darkness, perhaps intensified by it.

Hakim walks among them but not of them, the distance that age creates, the anthropological position that observes while participating minimally, enough to avoid suspicion, not enough to be included. The sea is audible but barely visible, its presence announced through sound—waves continuous but irregular, the arhythmic rhythm that consciousness tries to pattern, fails, tries again, the repetition without exact repetition that defines natural processes, that distinguishes them from mechanical reproduction, from the industrial consistency that modernity mistakes for perfection.

The stars have achieved full visibility, as full as light pollution permits, the astronomical loss that urbanization requires, accepts, and forgets to mourn. Orion rises in the east, the constellation that ancient Egyptians associated with Osiris, that Greeks saw as hunter, that astronomy recognizes as asterism, chance alignment from Earth's perspective, the stars actually at different distances, unrelated except through projection, the meaning consciousness creates from random distribution, the patterns that exist only in perception, from particular position, at particular time, the cosmic accident of viewpoint that makes meaning possible, necessary, false.

> Night is not day's absence but a different presence, not negation but alternative, the processes that darkness enables, requires— sleep, dreams, the nocturnal ecology, the crimes and consolations that light inhibits.

Consciousness evolved for daylight, struggles with darkness, fears it appropriately, the vulnerability that unconsciousness creates, that sleep demands, the daily rehearsal of death that rest requires, that bodies insist upon despite the mind's resistance. We are diurnal temporarily, nocturnally, the third of life spent unconscious, the processes continuing without awareness—circulation, respiration, digestion, the autonomic functions that preceded consciousness, that enable it, that will outlast it briefly when brain ceases but body continues, the minutes or hours when blood still circulates through dead tissue, when cells continue metabolizing until oxygen depletes, when death proceeds gradually, systematically, the process that medicine can now reverse partially, temporarily, the boundary become zone, area rather than line.

A group of teenagers has assembled around someone's phone, watching a video that produces collective laughter, the shared screen that creates temporary community, the mediation that brings together while keeping apart, each viewing from a slightly different angle, receiving a different image, the parallax that makes every experience unique despite sharing the source. They don't notice Hakim passing, their attention absorbed, captured, the attention economy that extracts value from consciousness, that monetizes awareness, that makes a product from what was process, a commodity from what was capacity.

The notebook remains in the apartment but memory records, processes, begins the forgetting that is also transformation, the selective retention that creates narrative from experience, meaning from randomness, the story consciousness tells itself about what happened, which is never what happened but what needed to happen for consciousness to continue, to maintain coherence that might be illusion but is necessary illusion, functional fiction, the lie that enables truth or at least continuation.

An old woman sits alone on a bench, feeding cats that emerge from shadows, approach cautiously, accept food while maintaining distance, the calibrated trust that street animals develop, that enables survival without domestication. She speaks to them, the monologue that is also a dialogue, the cats responding through presence if not language, the interspecies communication that doesn't require a shared code, that operates through gesture, positioning, the embodied knowledge that preceded language, that remains when language fails.

"They remember," she says, noticing Hakim noticing, including him involuntarily in her practice. "Each night, same time, same place. They know I'll come. I know they'll come. This is all a relationship requires—reliable presence, mutual recognition, the pattern that continues until it doesn't."

Until it doesn't. The phrase that acknowledges termination without specifying it, that recognizes ending as possibility, probability, certainty eventually, but not yet, not tonight, the continuation that is always temporary but is temporary for now, the now that is all consciousness actually has despite memory's claim on past, anticipation's claim on future, the present that is present only briefly, immediately becoming past, the moment that exists only in passing, that cannot be held, examined, possessed, only experienced in its vanishing, its transformation into memory that is already interpretation, already fiction, already lost.

The darkness has deepened, the transition complete enough that eyes have adapted, pupils dilated, rhodopsin regenerated, the chemistry of vision adjusted for scotopic conditions though scotopic is relative, the city never achieving true darkness, the light pollution that makes astronomy impossible, that erases stars, that replaces cosmos with streetlights, the trade that urbanization requires, the loss that most don't recognize as loss, having never known true darkness, the darkness that reveals the Milky Way, the galaxy's edge-on view, the billions of stars that surround us, that we're part of, that consciousness emerged from, temporarily, accidentally, magnificently, meaninglessly, meaningfully.

He continues walking, eastward again, the circuit approaching completion though completion is arbitrary, the starting point being chosen not given, the boundary that consciousness creates then treats as real, as significant, the meaning-making that can't be stopped, that might be consciousness's essence if consciousness has essence, which process philosophy denies, insisting on process not essence, becoming not being, the verbal preference that might be mere preference or might be recognition of something fundamental, something that substance metaphysics misses, mistakes, the error that millennia of philosophy have sustained, that process thought attempts to correct, perhaps overcorrects, the pendulum swinging from substance to process, missing the middle that might not exist, the balance that might be impossible.

A man approaches, drunk or tired or both, his gait irregular, compensating, the body maintaining balance despite impairment, the proprioceptive intelligence that operates below awareness, that keeps us upright, oriented, the vestibular system that evolved from fish's lateral line, the gravity sensors that work continuously, unconsciously, the background processing that consciousness depends on but doesn't acknowledge, like the heart's beating, like the liver's filtration, like the kidneys' regulation, the processes that continue whether attended or not, that attention might disrupt, that function best when forgotten.

"Doctor," the man says, the identification unclear—does he recognize Hakim specifically or identify him as type, the class markers that persist despite attempted erasure, the habitus that Bourdieu described, the embodied cultural capital that announces itself through posture, gesture, the subtle signals that locate individuals socially, economically, and educationally.

"I'm not practicing," Hakim responds, the clarification that is also a deflection, the boundary setting that urban interaction requires.

"No one is practicing," the man responds, the statement cryptic, philosophical perhaps or perhaps just drunk wisdom, the profundity that intoxication sometimes enables, sometimes mimics, the altered consciousness that might access different truths or might just be altered, the consciousness that is always already altered anyway, by culture, by language, by the particular configuration of neurotransmitters, hormones, the chemistry that makes experience possible, that makes experience particular, that ensures no two consciousnesses experience identically, the solipsism that empathy attempts to bridge but can't, not fully, the gap that makes individuals individual, alone, together in aloneness.

The man continues past, the encounter brief, ambiguous, already becoming an anecdote, a story, the transformation of experience into narrative that consciousness performs continuously, compulsively, the story-making that might be adaptation, might be pathology, might be simply what this configuration of matter does under these conditions, the emergence that complexity enables, requires, the whole exceeding the sum of parts, consciousness exceeding neurons, meaning exceeding information, the excess that is everything or nothing depending on perspective, depending on what matters, what can matter, what we make matter.

> The sea at night is a different sea, not visually but auditorily, the sound carrying further in cooler air, the density differential that makes sound waves propagate differently, the physics that consciousness experiences as atmosphere, as mood, as the night's particular quality that is not mystical but physical, measurable, the decibels and frequencies that instruments detect, that consciousness interprets, that become experience, that become memory, that become the story of walking by the sea at night, the story that is not false but is not true either,

is something else, something between or beyond truth and falsity, the third category that experience occupies, that consciousness creates, inhabits, shares through language that translates experience into communicable form, losing everything essential, preserving everything essential, the paradox that communication is, that consciousness accepts, must accept to not be alone, to maintain the fiction of shared experience, shared meaning, shared world.

The apartment building approaches, or he approaches it, the question of who moves toward whom being relative, depending on reference frame, the physics that Einstein clarified but that consciousness still struggles with, the intuition that makes us geocentric, anthropocentric, egocentric, the center that is nowhere but seems to be wherever consciousness is, the privileged position that is not privilege but prison, the inability to escape our own perspective, to see from nowhere, to achieve the view that objectivity claims but can't deliver, the situated knowledge that is all knowledge despite pretensions otherwise.

But he doesn't enter, not yet, the night not yet exhausted, the body tired but consciousness alert, the dissociation that evening creates, that makes sleep difficult despite fatigue, the circadian disruption that modern life enables, electricity defeating darkness, screens defeating sleep, the evolutionary mismatch that makes insomnia epidemic, the inability to rest that capitalism produces, exploits, the twenty-four hour economy that never sleeps, that makes sleep seem like failure, weakness, the missing of opportunity, the fear of missing out that keeps consciousness vigilant, exhausted, unable to stop.

At the sea wall again, different position than morning, than afternoon, than evening, the same sea but different angle, different sound, the waves approaching from darkness, visible only at the last moment when streetlight catches foam, the white briefly brilliant then gone, swallowed by darkness that is not absence but presence of a different kind, the darkness that has mass, weight, the psychological experience of darkness as substance, as a thing rather than nothing, the phenomenology that contradicts physics but persists, the experience that is real regardless of accuracy, that makes darkness frightening, comforting, both, neither, depending on context, condition, the state of consciousness that encounters it.

> I came here seeking something, and found something else, the substitution that is not failure but education, the learning that occurs through disappointment, through the discovery that what we seek doesn't exist, never

existed except in imagination that projected onto world what world doesn't contain, can't contain, the meaning that must be made not found, the purpose that must be created not discovered, the hard wisdom that consciousness achieves or doesn't, that makes adulthood possible or impossible, that distinguishes maturity from mere aging, the acceptance that the universe doesn't care, can't care, that care is consciousness's addition, projection, gift to itself, the strange loop of meaning-making in meaningless cosmos, the defiance that is also submission, the rebellion that is also acceptance.

A couple passes, elderly, walking slowly, her hand through his arm, the support that is mutual, the balance achieved together that neither could maintain alone, the interdependence that age makes visible, that youth disguises, the fiction of independence that bodies maintain temporarily then surrender, the vulnerability that is a human condition despite technological mediation, despite medical intervention, despite the longevity that modernity provides some, denies others, the inequality that makes some bodies worth preserving, others disposable, the economics of life that capitalism calculates, that consciousness rejects but participates in, the complicity that contemporary existence requires.

They nod, the acknowledgment that night walkers exchange, the recognition of shared nocturnality, the choice to be out when convention suggests inside, the mild rebellion that walking at night represents, the claim to public space when public has retired, when space becomes different, charged with different possibilities, different dangers, the night that enables and threatens, that consciousness navigates carefully, alertly, the vigilance that darkness demands, that exhausts, that makes tomorrow's rest necessary, inevitable.

"The sea never sleeps," the old man says in passing, the observation offered without expecting response, the gift of recognition, of shared attention to what continues while consciousness pauses, the processes that don't require witness but receive it, temporarily, gratefully perhaps, though gratitude implies consciousness that the sea lacks, the anthropomorphism that language enables, requires, the metaphor that is an error but a necessary error, a functional mistake, the projection that makes world speakable, even if falsely.

Stars reflect on water when waves permit, the light that left those stars years, centuries, millennia ago arriving now, hitting retina, creating the experience of a star that might no longer exist, that probably has changed, moved, the light carrying information about a past that masquerades as a present, the temporal confusion that astronomy accepts, works with, the knowledge that what we see is what was, that present is inaccessible, that universe is experienced historically, through delay, the gap between the event and the perception that increases with distance, that makes cosmos archaeological, the past visible, the present invisible, and the future unknowable.

Death is certain but not tonight, probably, the calculation that consciousness makes continuously, unconsciously, the risk assessment that keeps us functional despite mortality's certainty, the denial that is not denial but postponement, the reasonable assumption that patterns will continue until they don't, that tomorrow will arrive for me though not for everyone, the statistics that make individual death unlikely while making collective death certain, the mathematics that consciousness can't fully grasp, that makes us act as if immortal while knowing we're mortal, the cognitive dissonance that enables planning, hoping, the future orientation that makes the present bearable, meaningful, despite the future's certainty of ending, of consciousness ceasing, of the processes that are me dispersing, transforming, continuing differently, without me, the me that is a pattern not a substance, that is a temporary coordination of processes that preceded me, that continue through me, that will continue after, the after that I won't experience, that is unimaginable despite imagination's efforts, the blank that death is for consciousness that can imagine everything except its own absence.

Time to return, to climb stairs one more time today, the repetition that makes routine, that makes place from space, that creates belonging through duration, even if belonging is fiction, projection, the meaning assigned rather than discovered. The door opens to darkness that familiarity makes navigable, the muscle memory that bodies develop, that makes motion automatic, efficient, the unconscious competence that frees consciousness for other tasks or for no task, for the rest that approaches, that demands submission, that consciousness resists until resistance fails, until exhaustion wins, until sleep arrives, departs, and arrives again, the cycle within cycle, the rhythm that bodies insist upon, that culture disrupts, that modernity makes difficult, that night enables despite electricity, despite screens, despite the attempt to make night into day, to eliminate darkness, to maintain consciousness continuously, the impossible project that fails nightly, that must fail for sanity, for health, for the processes that sleep enables, the memory consolidation, the cellular repair, the dreams that process what consciousness can't, that make sense from nonsense or nonsense from sense, the distinction unclear, perhaps meaningless.

The notebook opens one final time, the day demanding a conclusion, though conclusion is arbitrary, the boundaries consciousness create then treat as real.

The pen moves across paper, the marks that encode meaning, that will survive the consciousness that made them, briefly, the material trace that writing is, the death defying that is also death acknowledging, the attempt to persist through signs that outlast bodies, that communicate across time, that make past present for future consciousness that reads, interprets, misunderstands necessarily, the translation that reading is, that communication requires, that ensures meaning changes even when words remain stable, the process that writing initiates but doesn't control, can't control, the release that publication is, the death that authorship requires, the meaning leaving maker, becoming other, becoming public, becoming process rather than product.

> Mediterranean night. The sea continues its circulation invisible, but continuing, the process that doesn't pause for darkness, that doesn't require light, that operates through forces that preceded consciousness, that will

outlast it. The day is complete—not concluded but complete in its incompletion, its partial view, its limited understanding, its temporary participation in processes that exceed comprehension but include it, permit it, enable the meaning-making that might be error, might be gift, might be simply what happens when matter organizes at this level of complexity, for this duration, under these conditions. Tomorrow there will be another dawn, another day, another opportunity to participate, to witness, to make meaning from patterns that need no meaning, that continue regardless, that include consciousness temporarily in their continuation, their process, their indifference that is not cruelty but freedom, the freedom that makes meaning possible because meaning is not given, required, the freedom that makes consciousness tragic and magnificent, temporary and necessary, impossible and actual. The sea doesn't remember today. I will remember for both of us, inaccurately, creatively, the memory that is not preservation but transformation, that makes past present, that enables future, that continues the process of processing, of participating, of being temporarily what processes provisionally produce, the pattern that coheres briefly then disperses, that calls itself *I*, that writes these words, that sleeps, dreams, wakes, continues until it doesn't, until the pattern dissolves, the processes continue differently, the sea remains.

The pen stops, final, sufficient. The notebook closes. The lamp extinguishes. Darkness returns, welcomed now, necessary, the darkness that is not ending but transition, the daily rehearsal for final darkness that will come, not tonight, probably not tomorrow, eventually certainly, the certainty that makes each day significant or insignificant, both simultaneously, the paradox that consciousness is, embodies, can't resolve, doesn't need to resolve, the tension that generates meaning, movement, the process that is life, that is consciousness, that is this day, complete.

Sleep approaches, consciousness beginning its dissolution, its temporary cessation, the processes continuing but awareness withdrawing, the mysterious transition from conscious to unconscious, the boundary that neuroscience maps but doesn't understand, the hard problem's nightly demonstration, the consciousness that somehow emerges from matter returning to matter, temporarily, reversibly, until the irreversible return, the final dissolution, but not tonight, tonight is sleep not death, process not conclusion, the continuation that tomorrow assumes, requires, enables.

The Mediterranean continues. Alexandria sleeps, mostly, the city's metabolism slowing but not stopping, the night shift workers, the insomniacs, the criminals, the lonely, maintaining minimal consciousness, keeping the city barely alive, ready for tomorrow's reanimation. Somewhere, dawn is breaking. Here darkness deepens.

The cycle continues. The process processes. The pattern persists, temporarily, sufficiently, necessarily, actually. This is enough.

SUN

# THE SUN THAT

# REMEMBERS

# DAWN

## LIGHT MEETS AWARENESS

The sun rose that morning with full knowledge that Hakim would never see it rise again.

Its light crept across the lake with unusual deliberation, as if savouring each moment of illumination, before spilling through the windows of the modest cabin where Hakim sat surrounded by his life's accumulation of questions.

Dust motes danced in the golden beams—miniature galaxies swirling above uneven stacks of spine-worn books in religion, science and philosophy that leaned on each other to chronicle humanity's ceaseless longing to understand.

He did not yet know what the sun knew, but something stirred in him with recognition, as if every sunrise he had ever witnessed had been preparing him for this one.

Hakim's ancestors, nomads and dreamers, wandered from the Near East to the land of the Nile centuries before his birth. Their blood carried stories older than the written word—tales of desert stars that spoke in silver tongues.

He, too, had departed west in a journey of discovery,

landing in sun-kissed prairies, wandering close to snow-capped mountains, moving toward vast oceans. Finally, he settled by this tranquil lake, drawn by something he could not name—a quality of light, perhaps.

He was not old by ordinary reckoning—just over sixty orbits around the sun—but the lines on his face told a different kind of age. Not the decay of time, but the erosion of certainty. Each wrinkle was a question that carved itself into flesh, each gray hair a hypothesis that withered under scrutiny. His eyes, deep-set and perpetually focused on distances others couldn't see, held the particular weariness of one who peered too long into microscopes and emerged wondering if the universe itself might be examining him with equal intensity.

For three decades, he studied cell biology in university laboratories and research hospitals. His specialty was the science of cellular rebellion. He became intimate with the ways cells could forget their origins and multiply without purpose. But between the careful observations and statistical analyses, questions began to creep in. Not scientific questions—those had clear methodologies for pursuit. These were different, more unsettling. The more he understood about the mechanics of life, the less he understood about life itself.

How could atoms arrange themselves into awareness? At what point did chemistry become experience? When did information processing become the feeling of wonder at a sunset or grief at a grave? These questions had driven

Hakim to this cabin by the lake. Not in retreat—but a space to think, to observe, to let questions ripen without forcing premature answers. His bookshelf revealed his journey. The bottom shelves held his scientific training: molecular biology texts with, volumes on biochemistry and genetics. The middle shelves showed his expansion: Schrödinger's "What Is Life?", Prigogine's work on dissipative structures, complexity theory, information theory, and quantum biology. And the top shelves held his current preoccupations: The Upanishads, Rumi's poetry, Ibn Arabi's "Bezels of Wisdom," Eckhart's sermons, along with contemporary works on consciousness—Chalmers, Nagel, Tononi and Kastrup.

It was not a rejection of science but an expansion beyond its self-imposed borders. Each book was a letter in an extended correspondence with mystery. Each page turned was another step on a spiral staircase that seemed to lead both inward and upward simultaneously.

Hakim rose from his desk, where he had been reading since before dawn—a passage from Ibn Arabi about the divine names manifesting through creation. He set the book down carefully, feeling a strange urgency to witness the sunrise.

The path to the lake was worn smooth by his daily pilgrimage. His feet found their way without conscious guidance, leaving his mind free to wander. The air carried autumn's first whisper, a mixture of death and promise that came when summer's green fire began its slow transformation into gold.

He settled onto the weathered granite boulder that had become his morning station. The stone still held yesterday's warmth in its depths while its surface had cooled to match the air—a lesson in how things could be multiple temperatures simultaneously, multiple truths existing in the same space. His body found the familiar depression worn by years of sitting, and he wondered idly if the stone had shaped him or he had shaped the stone, or if perhaps they had shaped each other in some conversation too slow for consciousness to track.

The eastern sky began its daily alchemy. First, the black softened to charcoal, then to ash, then to pearl. Venus still reigned in the lightening sky, but her sovereignty was numbered in minutes. The lake surface lay still as hammered pewter, holding its breath for the day's first wind. Somewhere behind the treeline, a bird offered a tentative note, testing the air's readiness for a song.

This was the moment Hakim treasured most—the pause between night and day, when reality seemed most malleable, most willing to reveal its deeper nature. He had read that many spiritual traditions considered dawn a "thin place," where the veil between worlds grew translucent. His scientific training had initially scoffed at such poetry, but years of observation had taught him that poetry often encoded truths too subtle for prose.

The horizon began to glow with rose and gold, colours

that had no names in any human language because they lasted too briefly for words to catch. The temperature shifted by degrees so fine that only skin could read them. His breath became visible in small puffs, each exhalation a visible reminder that he was chemistry in motion, combustion made conscious.

And then the sun's edge breached the horizon. In that instant, everything changed. The light hit Hakim's retinas and triggered the usual cascade of rhodopsin transformations, electrical impulses racing along his optic nerves, visual cortex activation—all the mechanical steps he could diagram from memory.

But something else happened too, something his training had no words for. *Time stuttered.*

The sun seemed to pause in its rising, as if catching sight of him and recognizing something it had been searching for across cosmic ages.

The light took on a quality of weight, of presence, of intent. *It didn't simply illuminate— it knew.*

Hakim's rational mind scrambled for explanations. Stroke? The symptoms didn't fit. Hallucination? But his vision remained crystal clear, arguably clearer than ever before. Every needle on every pine stood out in supernatural detail. Every ripple on the lake's surface seemed to carry meaning in its curves.

His heart began to beat with a rhythm that felt older than his body, as if it were synchronizing with some cosmic percussion that had always been there, waiting for him to hear it. His lungs drew air that tasted of eternity—not the sterile eternity of death but the pregnant eternity of the moment before creation speaks itself into being.

And then came the voice. Not sound—something deeper. Not words—something clearer. It arose from the same place dreams arose, the same depth from which love emerged, the same mystery that transformed chemicals into consciousness. It spoke with the authority of bedrock, the certainty of gravity, the finality of entropy:

*"This is the last sunrise."*

The message reverberated through every cell in his body, setting up harmonics in bones and blood.

His scientific mind tried to parse it, compartmentalize it and reduce it to manageable proportions.

Last sunrise? Was he dying? About to have a cardiac event? His hand moved instinctively to his chest, but his heartbeat, while strange, was strong. No pain, no numbness, none of the classical signs of immediate mortal danger.

But the voice—if voice it could be called—hadn't spoken of death. Not exactly.

It had spoken of completion, of cycles ending and beginning, of something his everyday language had no equipment to process.

It was like trying to understand the ocean from the perspective of a drop, trying to grasp symphony from the position of a single note.

His legs trembled, and he found himself sliding from the boulder to his knees on the dew-damp earth. Not in submission but in *recognition*.

Every sunrise he had ever witnessed—thousands of them—had been preparing him for this one. Every question he had asked had been a thread in a web that was only now revealing its pattern. Every cell he had studied, every book he had read, every night he had lain awake wondering about the nature of awareness—all of it had been approaching this moment with the inevitability of gravity.

The sun continued its rise, but Hakim no longer experienced it as an external event. The light seemed to be rising inside him as well, illuminating chambers of consciousness he hadn't known existed.

Memories flickered through his awareness—not his personal memories but something older, deeper. Images of caves and firelight, of temples and calculations, of laboratories and equations. As if he were remembering not just his own journey but the journey of consciousness itself as it had explored its own nature through billions of eyes across millennia.

The world around him began to shift. Not dramatically— more like the subtle adjustment of focus that transforms a collection of random dots into a three-dimensional image. The trees were still trees, but they were also something else— expressions of an urge toward light that was both physical and metaphysical. The lake was still water, but it was also a mirror, also memory, also the liquid thought of a planet dreaming.

His scientific training didn't rebel against these perceptions but expanded to accommodate them. He thought of quantum mechanics, where observation and phenomenon were inextricably intertwined. Of complexity theory, where simple rules gave rise to infinite expressions. Of information theory, where information and its physical substrate proved inseparable. Perhaps mysticism and mechanism were not opposites but different languages describing the same ineffable process.

The sun climbed higher, and with each degree of arc, Hakim felt layers of assumption peeling away like old paint. The careful categories he had used to organize experience— self and other, mind and matter, sacred and secular—began to reveal themselves as conveniences rather than truths. Useful for navigation but ultimately as provisional as the constellations, patterns imposed on stars that knew nothing of the shapes we traced between them.

A breeze arose from the lake, carrying the scent of pine resin and decay, growth and death intermingled in the endless recycling that was nature's deepest teaching. Hakim breathed it in, feeling his lungs exchange molecules with the world in the most intimate of dances. Where did his body end and the air begin? At what exact point did "outside" become "inside"? The questions that had once seemed philosophical now presented themselves as immediate, practical concerns.

He became aware of his posture—still kneeling on the earth, hands pressed against soil and stone. The granite boulder beside him no longer seemed like furniture but like family, shaped by the same forces that had shaped his bones, subject to the same laws that governed his thoughts. The moisture soaking through his pants knee wasn't separate from the blood in his veins—both were expressions of water's journey through various states and systems, temporary configurations of hydrogen and oxygen exploring the possibilities of form.

Time began to behave strangely. The sun's movement slowed to an imperceptible crawl, yet simultaneously, Hakim felt himself experiencing multiple moments at once. He was the child wondering at his first sunset, the young scientist peering through his first microscope, the middle-aged man reading philosophy by lamplight, the present self kneeling by the lake. All these Hakims existed simultaneously, like harmonics of a fundamental tone.

And beneath them all, supporting them like the drone note in a raga, was something that had no name because it preceded naming. It was the awareness that made all the other awarenesses possible, the knowing that knew the knowing. It had been there all along, patient as stone, constant as breath, waiting for him to stop looking elsewhere and recognize what had always been closest.

The message echoed again, not as words but as direct

understanding: This sunrise was last because it was first—the first one he was truly present for, truly conscious of.

All the others had been preparation, practice, prelude. This was the sunrise seeing itself through eyes it had fashioned from stardust and water for exactly this purpose.

Hakim felt tears on his cheeks, but couldn't say whether they were his or the morning dew or the lake itself weeping with recognition. The boundaries that had seemed so clear in the fluorescent light of laboratories were dissolving in this more ancient illumination. He was the observer and the observed, the question and the answer, the seeker and the sought.

As the sun cleared the treeline, its light struck the lake's surface and shattered into millions of diamonds, each one a small sun, each one containing the whole while remaining utterly itself. The metaphor was so perfect it ceased to be a metaphor. This was how consciousness worked—one light, infinite reflections, each point containing the whole while manifesting as the particular.

Hakim rose slowly, his knees protesting the prolonged contact with cold ground. But the discomfort felt like communication rather than complaint, his body reminding him that transcendence didn't mean escape from form but full presence within it. He was not having a spiritual experience that divorced him from the physical—he was discovering that the physical had always been spiritual, that matter had always been kin to mind, that the division between them was the first and last illusion.

He stood facing the sun, no longer able to maintain the fiction that he was separate from it. The photons striking his retinas had journeyed eight minutes through the vacuum of space to deliver their message, but their real journey had been far longer—from the first hydrogen fusion in the sun's core, before that from the gravitational collapse of cosmic clouds, before that from the Big Bang itself. He was stardust contemplating stars, the universe becoming conscious of itself through the unlikely miracle of organic chemistry.

The voice spoke again, and this time Hakim recognized it as his own deepest knowing, the part of him that had never forgotten what the rest of him had spent a lifetime trying to remember:

*"Dawn is for seeking, dusk for finding.*
*Between them, the seeker becomes the witness."*

He understood then that this day would be unlike any other. The sun's arc from dawn to dusk would trace a different kind of journey—one measured not in hours but in recognitions, not through space but through understanding. He would traverse not geography but the ways humans had tried to grasp the ungraspable mystery of their own awareness.

His body would remain here by the lake, but

consciousness would spiral through history—through philosophy, science, and mysticism—tracing every thread in the tapestry of humanity's search for itself. And when the sun completed its arc and touched the western horizon, he would finally understand what he had always been looking for: not an answer but a recognition, not a destination but a homecoming.

Hakim walked slowly back to his cabin, each step deliberate and weighted with finality. Inside, he made coffee with deliberate care, watching steam rise like incense, feeling warmth spread through the ceramic mug and into his hands with equal tenderness. He would not write yet—if words came, they would come later, after this quiet receiving was complete.

Outside, the sun continued its ancient arc, and Hakim sat in perfect stillness, no longer watching but participating. The books waited on their shelves. And somewhere between one breath and the next, the seeker dissolved into the witnessing, as natural and inevitable as light becoming sight.

# EARLY MORNING

## THE FIRST DREAMERS

As the morning light strengthened, filling his cabin with amber warmth, Hakim felt the first pull of dissolution. It began at the edges of vision, where peripheral awareness meets imagination, where the conscious mind releases its grip to deeper currents. The familiar walls of his study seemed to breathe, expanding and contracting with his own breath, until the distinction between internal and external space became meaningless.

*Then came the folding—not of space but of time itself.*

The scent hit him first: smoke, animal fat, ochre, sweat, blood and the musk of bodies that had never known soap. His nostrils flared with recognition that bypassed his personal memory entirely, reaching into cellular   archives before his species had words for remembering.

The walls dissolved, replaced by stone that flickered with shadow and flame. He was in a cave, but not as a visitor—as participant, as one who belonged to this darkness and firelight as completely as he had ever belonged anywhere. The cave walls pulsed with images painted in earth pigments: bison with eyes that seemed to track movement, horses caught mid-gallop, the negative spaces of human hands pressed against stone like signatures on a cosmic contract.

Around the fire sat his tribe—not his ancestors by blood alone but by something deeper. They wore the skins of animals they had thanked before killing, their faces painted with designs that were both decoration and invocation. Their eyes held a quality of attention he recognized from his years of scientific observation, but directed toward different mysteries.

An old woman tended the fire with movements that carried the weight of ritual. Each placement of wood, each stirring of coals followed patterns passed down through generations beyond counting. She was the keeper of more than flame—she was the one who remembered which plants healed and which killed, which stars marked the migration of herds, which songs could call rain or settle the spirits of the dead. Her knowledge lived not in books but in her bones, encoded in gesture and breath.

Beside her, a young man worked flint with patient percussion, each strike calibrated by feel rather than theory. The stone spoke to him through vibration and resistance, revealing its hidden planes of cleavage, its willingness to become a tool. He wasn't imposing form on matter—he was conversing with it, finding the spear point that already existed within the stone, waiting to be released.

But it was the painter who drew Hakim's deepest attention. She stood before a section of cave wall where firelight and shadow created a natural canvas. Her fingers were stained with ochre—red as blood, yellow as sun, black as the space between stars. She studied the rock's surface with the intensity of a scientist preparing an experiment, but her purpose was different. She wasn't trying to represent— she was trying to invoke.

When she finally moved, it was with the certainty of one who had received instructions from sources beyond human consultation. Her hand swept across the stone, leaving the outline of a bison's hump. Another movement birthed a horn, then an eye that seemed to open as she drew it. The image emerged not as a copy but as a capture—she was binding something essential about the bison into the stone, creating a connection that would allow her people to touch the animal's spirit even when the herds were distant.

Hakim understood with a shock of recognition: this was humanity's first technology of consciousness. Not the spear or the fire, revolutionary as those were, but the *ability to take inner experience and give it outer form*. The painting wasn't decoration or even representation—it was a tool for accessing the numinous, for keeping the dialogue between human and more-than-human worlds open and flowing.

The painter stepped back, and others approached the image. They didn't simply look—they participated. An old man placed his palm against the painted bison and closed his eyes, his lips moving in what might have been a prayer or conversation. A child traced the outline with one finger, learning through touch what the eyes alone couldn't convey. The image had become a *portal*, a place where the membrane between inner and outer grew permeable.

Language here was different—not the complex symbolic system Hakim knew, but something more immediate, more embodied. They spoke in fluid gestures, in tones that carried meaning below the level of words, in shared silences that communicated more than speech. When they did use what might be called words, these were less labels than invocations—sounds that didn't simply point to things but participated in their essence.

A man returned from hunting, and his arrival sparked a transformation in the cave's atmosphere. He didn't need to announce success or failure—his body told the story in its posture, its rhythm, its scent. The others read him like a text written in flesh and movement. When he began to move in what modern eyes might call dance, he wasn't performing— he was transmitting. His body became the hunt itself, every gesture encoding crucial information about the behaviour of prey, the lay of the land and the presence of predators.

The others joined him, not in imitation but in expansion. Each body added its own thread to the narrative, weaving a collective understanding that no single perspective could achieve. An elder's movements showed how the herds had moved in other years, a woman's gestures indicated where healing plants grew along the migration route, a youth's energetic leaps suggested new strategies for the kill.

Hakim realized he was witnessing the birth of what would later be called culture, but here it was *inseparable* from nature. These people didn't see themselves as living "in" an environment—they were *participants* in a vast, ongoing conversation where every element had voice and agency. The river spoke through its seasonal changes, the sky through its patterns of cloud and clear, the earth through what it chose to grow or withhold. And humans spoke back, not as masters but as one voice in a cosmic chorus.

Death here wore a different face than in Hakim's world. When an elder lay dying, the tribe gathered not in desperate medical intervention but in accompaniment. They sang the dying one across the threshold, their voices creating a bridge of sound between states of being. The body would be returned to earth or sky with ceremonies that suggested not ending but *transformation*—the same consciousness that had animated the human form dispersing back into the larger awareness from which it had temporarily crystallized. Hakim watched a child's initiation into deeper mysteries.

The boy had reached the age where childhood's unconscious participation must give way to conscious relationship. The shamans—for lack of a better word—prepared him through fasting and isolation, thinning the veils of ordinary perception until he could perceive what was always there but usually ignored.

When they finally led him to a sacred site—a grove where trees grew in a perfect circle, their branches interweaving overhead like neural networks—the boy's eyes held the particular terror and wonder of one about to lose the comfort of a smaller identity. The ritual that followed was simultaneously brutal and tender, stripping away the child's ego-boundaries while surrounding him with the tribe's collective support.

They used sacred plants—teachers, they called them—that opened doorways in consciousness. Not for entertainment or escape but for education in the deepest sense. Under their influence, the boy experienced himself as a tree, as a stream, as a hawk, as a stone. Not metaphorically but directly, his consciousness expanded beyond the borders of skin to taste what existence felt like from other perspectives. When he returned to ordinary awareness, he carried maps of territory that couldn't be reached by foot alone.

This was education in its original sense—not the filling of an empty vessel but the leading out of innate knowing. The boy learned that consciousness wasn't his private possession but a community resource, a field in which all beings participated according to their nature. His human gift was not superiority but responsibility—the ability to be aware of awareness itself, to serve as witness and voice for the larger dreaming.

Hakim felt tears on his cheeks as he recognized what

had been lost. Not the specific practices—those had evolved for good reasons. But the fundamental recognition that consciousness was *ecology*, that awareness existed not in isolated packets but as a field phenomenon in which every being participated. These ancestors hadn't needed to solve the "hard problem of consciousness" because they'd never created it. They lived in a world where inner and outer reflected each other perfectly, where dream and wake were different modes of the same reality, where the human task was not to master but to maintain relationship.

A woman began to sing, and her voice carried the particular quality of truth that transcends language. She sang of the first fire, stolen from the sky-beings by Crow, who paid for the theft with his burned feathers. She sang of the agreement between human and animal, how the prey offered itself to the hunter who approached with proper reverence. She sang of the plants that chose to be medicine, the stones that consented to be tools, the trees that dreamed themselves into shelters.

The fire burned lower, and shadows danced on the cave walls, making the painted animals seem to move with life of their own. Or perhaps they did move—in this state of expanded awareness, Hakim couldn't maintain the rigid distinction between representation and reality that his scientific training insisted upon. The paintings were both symbol and substance, both map and territory, both human creation and independent entity.

He understood now why the first art had been sacred art. These images weren't early attempts at representation that would eventually evolve into photographic realism. They were technologies for maintaining contact with the numinous, for keeping the channels open between human consciousness and the larger awareness in which it swam. Every hand pressed against stone, every animal captured in ochre was a prayer and promise:

*We remember.*
*We maintain the connection.*
*We hold our place in the greater dreaming.*

As dawn strengthened outside where his physical form still sat in the cabin, Hakim felt the cave beginning to fade. But before it dissolved entirely, the old woman by the fire looked directly at him across the millennia. Her eyes held no surprise at his presence—in the fluid time of vision, all moments existed simultaneously. She reached into a leather pouch and withdrew something, holding it out to him with a gesture that was both offering and challenge.

It was a stone, smooth from handling, with natural markings that suggested a face in profile. But as Hakim looked closer, the face shifted—now human, now animal, now something that preceded the division between them. The stone pulsed with warmth that had nothing to do with temperature, carrying within it the accumulated attention of generations who had held it, prayed with it, recognized it as a node where consciousness had crystallized into form. "*This is the first teaching,*" the woman said without words, her meaning arriving directly in his understanding. "*Before the word, before the thought, before the division—this. The knowing that knows itself through stone and star, flesh and flame. You have forgotten, but the memory lives in your cells. Remember.*"

The cave dissolved, but the warmth of the stone remained in Hakim's palm even as his awareness returned to the cabin. He looked down at his empty hand, still feeling the weight of what had been placed there. Not a physical object but a transmission, a seed of understanding that would unfold as his journey continued.

Outside, the sun climbed higher, its light shifting from golden to white. The lake surface had begun to dance with small waves as the morning breeze arose. A hawk circled overhead, riding thermals that were invisible but undeniably real—a perfect metaphor for the currents of consciousness that supported all awareness while remaining forever beyond direct perception.

Hakim understood that he had been shown the baseline, the original condition from which all human seeking had departed. Those cave dwellers hadn't been primitive—they had been complete, living in full participation with a conscious cosmos. Every development since—agriculture, civilization, science, philosophy—had been an attempt to recapture that completeness through increasingly complex means. But complexity itself had become a barrier, each new system of understanding adding another layer of separation between human consciousness and its ground.

He rose from his chair, muscles stiff from sitting, and walked to the window. The world outside looked the same but felt different, as if he were seeing it through ancient eyes overlaid on his modern perception. Every tree was both a botanical specimen and a breathing presence. Every bird is both a product of evolution and a messenger from realms that preceded division into physical and metaphysical.

The journey had begun in earnest. The cave painters had known through participation. But participation alone hadn't been enough—consciousness wanted to see itself from new angles, to explore its own depths through the mirror of manifest existence.

That exploration would require leaving the cave, leaving the circle of firelight, leaving the immediate participation for the longer journey through separation and return. It would require the birth of language that divided as well as connected, the rise of agriculture that promised security at the cost of direct relationship, the emergence of cities where humans would forget the stars and remember them and forget them again in endless cycles.

As morning approached its fullness, Hakim felt the next wave of dissolution approaching. The first teaching had been given. The journey into forgetting was about to begin.

# MID-MORNING

## SEPARATION BECOMES SPEECH

The dissolution came more swiftly this time, as if the barriers between states of consciousness had been permanently thinned. The morning light streaming through his cabin windows took on the quality of hammered gold, and within that light, Hakim felt himself pulled forward through millennia. Through the rise and fall of unnamed civilizations, through the slow discovery of seeds and seasons, through the first walls built to separate inside from outside, sacred from profane, us from them.

When the world reformed around him, he stood in blazing noon heat on a street paved with baked brick. The city rose before him like humanity's answer to mountains—

ziggurats climbing toward heaven in precise mathematical steps, each level a mediation between earth and sky. This was Babylon, not the fallen city of later scripture but the living metropolis at its height, when it was the axis mundi of the known world.

The air shimmered with heat and human ambition. Merchants called their wares in a dozen tongues. Priests in white linen climbed the great ziggurat's steps, carrying offerings of grain and oil to the gods who lived in the high places. Scribes sat in whatever shade they could find, their styluses dancing across wet clay, transforming speech into marks that could outlive the speaker by millennia.

But beneath the commercial bustle and religious pageantry, Hakim sensed a profound shift in consciousness itself. These people no longer lived in the immediate participation he had witnessed in the cave. They had discovered *time*—not the cyclical time of seasons but historical time, time that accumulated, time that could be counted and controlled. They had discovered *law*, not the organic patterns of tribal custom but codified rules that applied regardless of relationship. They had discovered the *self*, not the fluid self that merged with tribe and cosmos, but the bounded self that could own property, make contracts and sin against absent gods.

He wandered through the city's quarters, observing how human consciousness had reorganized itself around new possibilities and new anxieties. In the temple complex, he watched priests performing rituals that had been formalized into precise liturgies. Every gesture was prescribed, every word written in sacred texts. The spontaneous invocation of the cave painters had evolved into spiritual technology, reliable and repeatable but more distant from its source.

A young priest explained the cosmic order to a group of initiates, using a clay model of the universe—earth below, heavens above, waters surrounding all. "The gods have withdrawn to their celestial palaces," he intoned.

"They no longer walk among us as in the ancient days. We must send our prayers upward through the proper channels, using the correct formulations, at the auspicious times determined by the movement of stars."

Hakim recognized the birth of *mediation*—the idea that divine consciousness was no longer directly accessible but required intermediaries, interpreters, technologies of ascent. The ziggurat itself was such a technology, a human-made mountain allowing priests to climb closer to gods who had retreated to untouchable heights. But each step upward was also a confession of distance, an acknowledgment that the immediate presence known to the cave dwellers had been replaced by hierarchical separation.

In the scribal schools, young boys learned to press wedge-shaped marks into clay, transforming the fluid continuum of speech into discrete units of meaning. Hakim watched one teacher drilling his students in the creation of contracts—so many measures of barley borrowed, to be repaid at such and such interest, with these penalties for default. Language, which had once invoked presence, was becoming a tool for managing absence. Words no longer participated in what they named but stood apart from it, *manipulating* reality through *symbolic* representation rather than direct engagement.

"See how the same mark can mean 'day' or 'sun' or 'brightness' depending on context," the teacher explained, his reed stylus dancing across a practice tablet. "The gods gave us writing so that their words could be preserved without distortion, so that law could be permanent, so that memory could be made solid."

But Hakim saw the shadow side of this gift. Writing created the possibility of lying in new ways, of creating false records, of manipulating memory itself. It froze the living flow of oral tradition into fixed forms that could be owned, hoarded and used as weapons. Most profoundly, it created the illusion that consciousness could be captured in marks, that the ineffable could be made effable through sufficient elaboration of script.

In the marketplace, he observed the birth of abstract value. Sheep were no longer just sheep—they were units of exchange that could be converted into silver, which could be converted into labour, which could be converted into status. The direct reciprocity of gift and counter-gift that had governed the cave dwellers' economy was being replaced by calculated exchange mediated by symbolic tokens. People were learning to think in abstractions, to manipulate mental representations of reality rather than engaging with reality directly.

A merchant showed him clay tokens used for accounting—spheres for measures of grain, cones for small units of oil, complex shapes for more valuable goods. "Before these, we had to trust memory and reputation," the merchant explained. "Now we have proof. Numbers don't lie."

But numbers, Hakim understood, also didn't tell the whole truth. They created a parallel universe of quantity that gradually eclipsed the universe of quality. A thousand sheep represented by marks on clay were not the same as a thousand sheep known individually, with their particular temperaments and histories. The gain in cognitive control came at the cost of intimate knowledge.

It was in the religious quarter that Hakim encountered the figure who would crystallize his understanding of this transition. The man didn't look like a prophet or a priest— his clothes were those of a merchant, his hands stained with the ink of commerce rather than the blood of sacrifice. But his eyes held a quality Hakim recognized from the cave painter, the old woman by the fire—the look of one who had touched something beyond the reach of common sight.

The man sat in the shade of a date palm, surrounded by a small group of listeners—not the wealthy or the powerful but workers, slaves, foreigners, those whom the great machinery of civilization had pushed to its margins. He was telling a story, but it was unlike the official myths proclaimed from temple heights. This was quieter, more intimate, more dangerous.

"In the beginning," he said, his voice carrying the rhythm of one who had learned his tales not from tablets but from desert nights, "there was no beginning. There was only the One, alone with Itself, containing all possibilities but knowing none of them. And the One gazed into the mirror of Its own being and saw... what? Not another, for there was no other. Not Itself, for there was no self to see. It saw the possibility of seeing, the potential for knowledge, the seeds of every story that would ever be told."

The listeners leaned in, recognizing something in these words that the official theologies had forgotten. This wasn't about gods who demanded grain and gold, who grew angry at improper rituals, who played favourites. This was about something more fundamental—the mystery of consciousness itself, knowing itself through the multiplicity of forms.

"And the One breathed," the storyteller continued, "and that breath became wind and word, sky and speech. And the One dreamed, and that dream became earth and all that grows from earth. Not creation from outside, like a potter shaping clay, but creation from within, like a seed unfolding into a tree. The One became many not by division but by expression, the way a single light becomes countless colours through a prism."

Hakim felt the hair rise on his arms. Here, in the heart of humanity's first great civilization, was someone trying to recover the participation mystique of the ancestors while acknowledging the irreversible journey into complexity. The storyteller wasn't rejecting the achievements of civilization—law, writing, mathematics and organized religion. He was trying to remember what they were for, what they pointed toward, what they could never quite capture.

"They tell you the gods have withdrawn," the man said, gesturing toward the ziggurat looming over the city. "They tell you that you need priests to speak for you, sacrifices to appease divine anger, proper words in proper order to gain divine favour. But I tell you the secret the priests have forgotten: the Divine never withdrew. It simply hid in plain sight."

A scribe in the crowd objected, "But without law, there is chaos. Without proper worship, the gods send drought and plague. Without distinction between sacred and profane, everything becomes contaminated."

The storyteller smiled with compassion. "I don't say abandon law, but remember what law serves. Don't cease your prayers, but recall who truly hears them. The separation you fear has already occurred—not in the world but in your sight. The holy never left. You did."

The crowd grew uncomfortable. Such words challenged not just religious doctrine but the entire structure of civilization built on separation and hierarchy. If everyone was a temple, what need for priests? If the Divine was equally present in the palace and the slum, what justified the vast inequalities of urban life? If consciousness was the fundamental ground rather than the exclusive possession of gods and kings, how could the social order maintain itself?

Sensing their unease, the storyteller shifted to a different register. "I don't say tear down the temples. I say remember what they represent. Each ziggurat is humanity's memory of the sacred mountain where heaven touched earth. But the touching hasn't ceased—you've simply stopped noticing. Each ritual recalls the original compact between consciousness and form. But the compact renews itself with every breath, every heartbeat and every moment of awareness."

He stood, preparing to leave, but offered one final teaching. "You know the story of the confusion of tongues, how humanity was scattered for trying to build a tower to heaven? The priests say it was punishment for hubris. But I tell you the deeper meaning: the One became many languages so It could discover how many ways there are to say 'I Am.' The scattering wasn't fall but flowering. Each people, each tongue, each way of knowing reveals another facet of the infinite diamond of consciousness."

As the man walked away, his listeners dispersed, but Hakim saw how his words had planted seeds. Some would dismiss them as the ravings of a mystic. Others would report them to authorities as potential heresy. But a few would carry them in their hearts, would begin to look for the Divine not just in designated sacred spaces but in the play of light on water, the laughter of children, the mystery of their own awareness.

The vision began to shift, and Hakim found himself moving through time within the same sacred geography. He saw a man leaving Ur, carrying not just his household but a new conception of divinity—not many gods embedded in natural forces but One God. He saw another in Egypt, where the same ancient wisdom was encoded in different symbols, receiving a revelation that would transform a tribal deity into a universal principle. He saw prophets and sages, each trying to recall humanity to its original recognition while adapting to the increasing complexity of civilized consciousness.

But he also saw the hardening, the institutionalization, the way each fresh revelation became fossilized into dogma. The liberating recognition that consciousness was One became the dividing insistence that only one way of recognizing it was valid. The inclusive mystery became exclusive possession. The pathways meant to lead back to participation became barriers preventing it.

As the vision faded and Hakim's awareness began returning to his cabin by the lake. The sun outside his window had climbed higher, approaching its zenith. The morning's journey through humanity's childhood was nearing its end. Soon, he would be shown how consciousness had tried to know itself through reason, through philosophy, through the systematic doubt that would strip away everything uncertain in search of bedrock truth.

But first, he needed to integrate what he had seen. The cave painters had shown him consciousness in its primordial unity. Babylon had shown him consciousness, its capacity for separation and self-reflection. Each stage was necessary, each carried gifts and losses. The question wasn't how to return to the cave—that was neither possible nor desirable. The question was how to carry forward the cave's recognition while embracing civilization's achievements.

The morning was advancing. Next, would come the philosophers, trying to capture the infinite in concepts, to build ladders of logic tall enough to reach heaven. The journey continued, but he was beginning to understand that arrival and departure were the same door seen from different sides. The sun that rose, knowing he would never see it rise again, was the same sun that had always risen, would always rise, in the eternal now where all moments existed simultaneously. He was ready for the next teaching.

# LATE MORNING

## THE MIRROR OF TWO WORLDS

The late morning sun had taken on a quality of crystalline clarity, each ray seeming to carry not just light but intelligence. Hakim felt the familiar dissolution beginning again, but this time it was gentler, like sinking into warm water that gradually became indistinguishable from his own substance. The boundaries of his cabin flickered and reformed, and he found himself in a garden that seemed to exist at the intersection of earth and heaven.

This was not the wild paradise of the cave painters or the engineered order of Babylon, but something altogether different—a garden built according to the principles of sacred geometry, where every path and fountain, every flowerbed and fruit tree was positioned to reflect cosmic harmonies. The air itself seemed to shimmer with mathematical precision, as if the space were constructed from pure ratios made visible.

At the garden's heart sat a figure in white robes, bent over a manuscript illuminated with diagrams that seemed to move and breathe on the page. His face carried the particular intensity of one who had spent decades pursuing a single question through labyrinths of logic and libraries of learning. Around him lay the accumulated wisdom of centuries—translated Greek philosophy,

Hindu mathematics carried on trade routes, Persian mysticism encoded in poetry, all flowing together in this moment when an emerging civilization was the world's great synthesizer of knowledge.

Hakim approached and saw that the manuscript was not one text but many, overlapping and interpenetrating—Aristotle's logic annotated with revealed verses, Platonic geometry expanded through algebraic innovations, medical observations intertwined with metaphysical speculation. This was the work of a polymath in an age when all knowledge was still one knowledge, before the great dividing that would separate science from philosophy from theology. "Tell me," the philosopher said, gesturing to a rose blooming  nearby, its petals arranged in a perfect spiral,

"What do you see?"

Hakim looked carefully. "A rose. Beautiful in its form, pleasant in its fragrance."

"Yes, but look deeper. What do you truly see?"

Hakim let his vision soften, allowing the rose to reveal more of itself. "I see... patterns. Mathematical relationships. The golden ratio in the spiral of petals. "The philosopher smiled. "Deeper still."

And then Hakim saw it—not with his physical eyes but with the organ of perception that the Sufis called the eye of the heart. The rose was not simply exhibiting mathematical properties. It was mathematics made manifest. The ratios and relationships weren't imposed on matter from outside but were the very language through which matter spoke itself into being.

"Now you begin to see," the philosopher said. "Everything reflects. That is the first principle of true science. The rose reflects beauty—not as a mirror reflects an image but as a child reflects its parent, carrying the essence forward into new expression. It participates in Beauty itself, the divine name "the Beautiful", not by representing it but by being a unique mode of its self-expression."

He gestured to the fountain at the garden's center, where water rose and fell in patterns that seemed to contain all possible movements. "Water reflects the divine name, the Ever-Living, through its constant motion and adaptation. It takes the shape of any container while remaining essentially itself. Is this not how consciousness moves through forms?" Hakim felt understanding dawn—not the intellectual understanding of concepts but the direct recognition, the tasted knowledge. This philosopher was not merely cataloging correspondences between earthly and heavenly things. He was describing a universe where every phenomenon was a theophany, a self-disclosure of divine attributes through material forms.

"Come," the philosopher said, rising with surprising grace for one who had clearly spent years in contemplation. "Let me show you the observatory."

They walked through the garden, past herbs arranged

according to their medicinal properties, past fruit trees whose branches had been trained into living calligraphy spelling out divine names. The path itself was a teaching, moving from the outer courts of sense experience toward the inner sanctum of intellectual vision.

The observatory was a dome of white marble inlaid with lapis lazuli in patterns that mapped the celestial sphere. Instruments of brass and silver stood ready to measure the movements of planets, the angles of stars, and the precise moments of eclipse and conjunction. But Hakim sensed these tools served a purpose beyond what would later be called astronomy.

"The moderns will separate science from sacred knowledge," the philosopher said, adjusting an astrolabe with practiced hands. "They will think they honour truth by stripping it of meaning. But we know better. The movements of the spheres are not mere mechanics—they are the cosmic dance of divine names in perpetual conversation."

He pointed to a chart showing the planetary orbits. "Each sphere is governed by an intelligence—not the superstitious star-gods of the ancients but conscious principles that mediate between the One and the many. The moon governs growth and decay, making manifest the divine names, the Giver of Life and the Bringer of Death. The sun reveals, the Light, not as metaphor but as reality—for what is physical light but the sensible manifestation of the Light of lights?"

Hakim studied the charts, seeing in them not the clockwork universe of later centuries but something more organic—a cosmos that was alive at every level, where consciousness wasn't an anomaly but the fundamental substrate expressing itself through infinite forms. The Greek conception of *nous*, divine intellect, had met the revelation of God's signs in nature, producing a vision where every natural phenomenon was both fully itself and fully symbolic of principles beyond itself.

"But here is the crucial recognition," the philosopher continued, leading Hakim to a smaller chamber where mirrors had been arranged in complex patterns. "Stand here, at the center."

Hakim positioned himself where indicated and gasped. The mirrors created an infinity of reflections, each showing him from a different angle, each slightly different yet undeniably the same person. But as he looked deeper, he saw that the reflections weren't simply bouncing light—they were revealing something about the nature of consciousness itself.

"This is the secret of existence," the philosopher whispered. "The One desired to be known, so It created the cosmos as a mirror for Its own infinite qualities. But a simple mirror would show only the surface. So it created conscious beings—humans, angels, perhaps others we cannot imagine—as polished mirrors capable of recognizing what they reflect."

"You are not merely material," he continued, his voice

taking on the quality of transmission. "Nor are you purely spiritual. You are the isthmus between worlds, the meeting place of heaven and earth. In you, matter becomes capable of contemplation.

Hakim felt vertigo, not of the body but of the self. If he was a mirror for divine self-contemplation, what was the "he" that seemed to be doing the mirroring? The philosopher sensed his question. "This is where logic reaches its limit and another kind of knowing begins. You cannot think your way to this recognition—you must be polished until it reflects itself in you. The rational soul can climb very high through demonstration and argument. But the final recognition comes only through divine self-disclosure to the heart that has been prepared to receive it."

They returned to the garden, where afternoon light was beginning to slant through the leaves, creating patterns of illumination and shadow that seemed to encode meanings just beyond intellectual grasp. The philosopher opened another manuscript, this one filled with geometric proofs.

"Let me show you how the ancients encoded this wisdom. They spoke of emanation—not creation in time but the eternal procession of existence from the One through various levels of being. First, the Universal Intellect, containing all forms in pure potentiality. Then the Universal Soul setting these forms in motion. Then the spheres, then the elements, then the compounds, ascending through minerals, plants, animals, to humans."

He traced the levels with his finger, showing how each stage was both an effect of what came before and a cause of what came after. "But here's the key insight—this isn't a linear chain but a circle. Humans, through consciousness, can ascend back through all these levels to reunite with their source. The mineral in you remembers its origin. The plant nature in you grows toward light. The animal soul in you seeks and flees. And the rational soul in you can recognize all these as modes of the One Life living itself through infinite forms."

"Is this not heretical?" Hakim found himself asking. "Does this not erase the distinction between Creator and creation?" The philosopher smiled with the patience of one who had faced this question many times. "Only if you think crudely. *The ocean is not the wave, yet the wave is nothing but ocean.* The sun is not its rays, yet the rays are nothing but the sun's light extending itself. The One transcends all forms, while being closer to them than they are to themselves. Both are true, and the tension between them is where consciousness lives."

He pulled out a treatise on optics, showing how he had investigated the behaviour of light through experimental methods that would later be called scientific. "Light travels in straight lines, reflects at equal angles, and refracts according to precise laws. But what is light? Not just particles or waves, but the physical symbol of knowledge itself. When you see, light from the object meets light from your eye, outer and inner illumination joining to create perception. Is this not how all knowledge works? The light of the intellect meeting the intelligible forms of things?"

Hakim marvelled at how this thinker wove together what would later be separated into hostile camps. Experimental observation served contemplative insight. Mathematical precision revealed mystical truths. The study of nature was a form of worship, each discovery a new verse in the ongoing revelation of reality.

As the day progressed toward noon, the philosopher led Hakim to one final location—a simple room with whitewashed walls. "All our learning, all our philosophy, all our science—it means nothing if it doesn't polish the mirror of the heart. The Greeks gave us logic, the Indians gave us mathematics, and the Persians gave us poetry. But the final teaching is simpler: No reality but Reality."

The garden had taken on the pregnant stillness of noon, when shadows disappear and all things stand in their essential light. The philosopher turned to Hakim with eyes that seemed to see through centuries. "Your age will forget this integral vision. Knowledge will shatter into specialties. The sacred and secular will divorce. Science will explain the how but exile the why. Philosophy will grow abstract, mathematics mechanical, mysticism anti-intellectual. The mirror will break into countless fragments, each reflecting only a portion of the whole."

"But the breaking is also part of the pattern," he

continued. "The One becomes many to know Itself through infinite perspectives. Even forgetting serves remembering. Even separation serves union. The spiral path leads away to lead back, descends to ascend, dies to be reborn."

He handed Hakim a small mirror of polished metal. "Keep this—not the object but what it represents. You are consciousness reflecting on itself. Polish yourself through knowledge, through devotion, through service, through contemplation. But remember—the polishing is not to become something you're not. It's to reveal what you've always been."

The vision began to fade, the garden becoming translucent, the philosopher's form dissolving into light. But his final words rang clear: "Ibn Arabi will come after me and speak of the Unity of Being. Others will call it heresy. But you who have tasted, you know—consciousness is not divided though it appears through infinite forms. The sun's light is one whether it illuminates a palace or a prison. Know yourself, and you know your Lord."

Hakim found himself back in his cabin, the noon sun streaming through windows that now seemed like apertures in a cosmic observatory. His hand tingled with the memory of the mirror, though no physical object remained. He understood that he had been shown consciousness at a crucial juncture—when intellectual sophistication had reached heights that would not be matched for centuries, when science and mysticism still danced together, when the unity of knowledge reflected the Unity of Being.

But already in the philosopher's warnings, he had heard the coming dissolution. The integral vision would fragment. The mirror would shatter. Consciousness would explore what it meant to see itself as fundamentally divided, to experience itself as isolated subjectivity confronting alien objectivity.

He rose and walked to his bookshelf, pulling down his worn copy of Ibn Sina's "Book of Healing." The words that had once seemed abstract now pulsed with lived meaning. The necessary existent was not a logical concept but the immediate reality of awareness itself—that which cannot not be, the am-ness that precedes all qualification. And everything else, including his own sense of separate selfhood, was contingent—possible but not necessary, real but not self-subsistent, waves that existed only in relation to the ocean.

The sun had reached its zenith. The morning's journey through humanity's philosophical childhood was complete. Consciousness had shown itself knowing itself through myth, through revelation, through rational demonstration. But all these were still modes of participation, ways of being included in a meaningful cosmos. The great exclusion was about to begin—the exile of consciousness from its own ground that would make possible both modern science's triumphs and its peculiar blindness.

# MIDDAY

## MIND DIVIDES FROM MATTER

The zenith sun hung directly overhead, casting no shadows, as if the world had been flattened into two dimensions. This shadowless moment seemed to precipitate the next dissolution, pulling Hakim from the warmth of integrated wisdom into a colder, sharper clarity. The light itself changed quality—from the golden honey of contemplative noon to something more like winter starlight: brilliant but distant, illuminating but not warming.

When the world reformed, he found himself in a small, sparse room dominated by the smell of wood smoke and melting wax. Frost etched patterns on window panes, and beyond them, a European winter gripped the landscape in iron cold. The year was sometime in the early seventeenth century—Hakim could feel it in the quality of thought itself, poised at a fulcrum between medieval synthesis and modern analysis.

A figure sat hunched at a simple wooden desk, wrapped in a heavy cloak against the chill. Before him lay a piece of honeycomb wax, and he turned it slowly in the candlelight, studying it with the intensity of a man examining the fundamental nature of reality.

The figure was in the midst of the radical doubt that would reshape Western consciousness. He had stripped away every certainty, dismissed the testimony of his senses, questioned the reality of the external world, even entertained the possibility that an evil demon might be deceiving him about the nature of mathematics itself. And yet, in this abyss of skepticism, he had found one thing that couldn't be doubted.

"I think, therefore I am," he murmured in Latin, and Hakim felt the words land like an axe blow on the root of a tree. In that simple statement, the integral cosmos of the Islamic philosophers shattered. No longer was consciousness the unified field in which all phenomena arose. Now it was split—*res cogitans*, the thinking thing, trapped inside the skull, peering out at *res extensa*, the extended thing, the mechanical world of matter in motion.

Hakim watched as he continued his meditation on the wax. 'When cold, it has one set of properties—hardness, shape, colour, scent. When I bring it near the flame, all these change. Yet I know it remains the same wax. How? Not through the senses, which show me only changing qualities. Not through imagination, which cannot encompass all possible states of wax. Only through the intellect,  through pure reason, can I grasp the essence that persists through change.

It was brilliant, this isolation of rational thought as the one certainty. But Hakim could see what the philosopher couldn't—the devastating consequences of making thought the ground of being rather than being the ground of thought. By starting from isolated consciousness and trying to reason his way back to the world, he was creating a problem that would haunt philosophy for centuries: how does the ghost in the machine touch the machine?

The room grew colder, as if the philosophical ice age were manifesting physically. He pulled his cloak tighter and continued writing. "The body is a machine, marvellously complex but fully explicable through the laws of motion. Animals are automata, responding to stimuli through hydraulic pressures in their nerves. Even human bodies operate mechanically—only the rational soul, divinely implanted, distinguishes us from clockwork."

Hakim felt a chill deeper than winter. The living cosmos where every level of being participated in consciousness, was being murdered by logic, replaced with a dead mechanism occasionally haunted by isolated minds. The garden where matter and meaning intertwined was becoming a factory floor where blind forces pushed insensate particles according to mathematical laws.

The vision shifted, and Hakim found himself in a grand hall where natural philosophers demonstrated the new worldview. A lecturer stood before an elaborate mechanical model of the solar system—brass arms holding ivory spheres, gears meshing with perfect precision, the whole apparatus moving in elegant clockwork harmony.

"Behold," the lecturer proclaimed, "the cosmos stripped
of superstition! No longer do we need to invoke intelligences moving the spheres, sympathies and antipathies between elements, occult influences and formal causes. Everything reduces to matter in motion, particles pushing particles according to invariant laws. God, the supreme mathematician, has constructed a machine so perfect it requires no further intervention."

The audience—men in powdered wigs and elegant coats—applauded this triumph of reason over mystery. One called out, "But what of consciousness itself? How does matter in motion give rise to thought?"

The lecturer waved dismissively. "A problem for theologians, not natural philosophers. Our task is to map the mechanism. The soul's relation to it is beyond empirical investigation."

And there it was—the great *bifurcation* that would define the modern age. Consciousness was formally exiled from nature, relegated to a supernatural realm that science couldn't touch. The price of mechanical clarity was meaning itself.

The vision accelerated, showing Hakim the consequences cascading through time. The author of Principia describing a universe of forces and vectors where God was needed only as a first cause. Another declaring he had no need of the god hypothesis. The triumph of the mechanical philosophy in explaining everything except the explainer.

He saw laboratories where life itself was being reduced to mechanism. "See how the leg of this dead frog kicks when we apply electrical stimulation," a scientist demonstrated. "Life is nothing but chemical reactions and electrical impulses. Give us sufficient knowledge of the mechanism, and we shall create life from scratch."

But always, in the corner of every materialist triumph, stood the impossible fact of the observer. Who was watching the mechanism? What was the "I" that studied brains, the awareness that mapped matter? The mechanical philosophers had various strategies for ignoring this question—declaring it outside science's scope, reducing it to an emergent property that would eventually be explained, or simply pretending it wasn't there. But the ghost in the machine refused to be exorcised by denial.

Hakim found himself in another scene—a salon where the implications of mechanism were being worked out for human society. "If humans are machines," a philosophe argued, "then society can be engineered like any mechanism. Find the right laws, the correct arrangements of rewards and punishments, and you can create perfect order. Crime is malfunction. Virtue is proper operation. Freedom is the smooth running of well-oiled gears."

The shadow of this vision stretched forward—Hakim could see it darkening centuries to come. Humans as resources to be optimized. Education as programming.

Medicine as repair. Psychology as debugging. The rich, qualitative world of experience progressively reduced to quantities, measurements and manipulable variables.

Yet even as the mechanical worldview triumphed, cracks appeared in its edifice. Hakim watched a young philosopher walking in a garden, troubled by thoughts that wouldn't fit the mechanical mold. "If we are merely matter in motion," he mused, "how can we know truth? For truth implies a relation between thought and reality that mechanism cannot explain. A thought is not true because it's caused by certain  brain  states—causation and  truth  are different categories entirely."

And elsewhere, poets and mystics refused the exile of consciousness. Some raged against the 'sleep of reason' that mechanism imposed, seeing it as a kind of deadening enchantment. Others found in nature something that mechanism  couldn't  capture—'a  sense  sublime  of something far more deeply interfused.' The Romantics insisted that feeling and imagination revealed aspects of reality that reason missed.

But these were rearguard actions against the advancing mechanical tide. The split that had been initiated was widening into an abyss. On one side, the objective world fully describable by mathematics but drained of meaning. On the other, subjective consciousness rich with meaning but severed from causal efficacy. Two worlds that could never meet because the very framework that created them made their meeting impossible.

As noon passed into the afternoon, the vision began to fade. Hakim found himself back in his cabin, but the familiar space felt different. He was aware, as never before, of the dualistic assumptions built into the very structure of modern experience. The window that seemed to separate the inside from the outside. The sense of being a consciousness 'in here' looking at a world 'out there.' The habitual dividing of experience into subjective and objective poles.

He picked up a glass of water and drank slowly, feeling the liquid's coolness, its weight, its wetness. In the mechanical view, this was just H2O molecules interacting with nerve endings, creating electrochemical signals interpreted by the brain. But the actual experience—the quale of coolness, the satisfaction of thirst, the simple presence of water meeting awareness—where was that in the mechanism? It was nowhere because the mechanism had no place for it, could only ignore or explain it away.

Yet he was not simply rejecting mechanism. Its insights were real, its practical power undeniable. The error wasn't in seeing the mechanism but in seeing only the mechanism. The mistake wasn't in discovering that bodies operated according to physical laws but in forgetting that discovery itself transcended those laws. Consciousness didn't violate mechanism—it included and exceeded it, like a sentence includes and exceeds its grammar.

The afternoon sun slanted through his window, creating patterns of light and shadow that no equation could fully capture—not because equations were false but because they were abstractions, and reality was always richer than any abstraction. The mechanical theatre had shown consciousness one of its own faces—the face that could step back, analyze, manipulate and control. But in falling in love with this face, it had forgotten all the others.

Now the vision would deepen. Having split consciousness from the world, human thought would spend centuries trying to repair the breach through reason alone. The Enlightenment was dawning, and with it the magnificent and doomed attempt to make the isolated rational mind the measure of all things.

Hakim prepared himself for the next act in consciousness's self-discovering drama. The ghost in the machine was about to declare itself the only reality worth considering.

# AFTERNOON

## MATTER DISCOVERS MIND

The afternoon sun had begun its descent toward the western horizon, painting Hakim's cabin in shades of amber and rust. As the light shifted, so did the quality of time itself, accelerating as if consciousness were eager to show him how quickly certainties could crumble, how rapidly worldviews could reshape themselves once set in motion.

The dissolution came swift and sharp, like diving from sunlit surface into deeper currents. When Hakim emerged, he stood on a different shore—windswept, gray, where ancient bones littered the strand like discarded arguments. This was no tropical paradise but a harsh northern coast, where wind and wave had carved truth from stone with

patient violence.

A figure crouched among the rocks, notebook in hand, studying something with the total absorption Hakim recognized from his own laboratory years. But this was no indoor scientist—salt spray had weathered his face, his hands were rough from shipboard work, his eyes held depths that came from seeing too much of the world's strangeness.

The young naturalist, though still early in his career, was already marked by the quality that would define him—the ability to look without blinking at evidence that shattered comfortable assumptions. He was examining a fossilized shell embedded in the cliff face far above any current tide line, letting the implications settle into his bones before allowing them into his thoughts.

"The earth speaks," he murmured, not to Hakim but to himself, but in a language theology never taught. "These shells lived and died millions of years before Eden. These bones belonged to creatures no ark could hold. Either scripture lies, or it speaks in metaphors so vast we've missed the meaning entirely."

He stood, brushing sand from his trousers, and gazed out at the restless sea. "But if species aren't fixed creations but flowing processes, if forms bleed into one another across deep time, if life itself is a branching experiment with no predetermined outcomes... then what becomes of the soul? What becomes of purpose?"

Hakim felt the vertigo that the naturalist's contemporaries would soon experience. The mechanical universe had been cold but stable—a clock implied a clockmaker, even an absent one. But this new vision was far more unsettling. Life wasn't designed, but emerged. Complexity wasn't planned but accumulated. Consciousness wasn't divinely implanted but... what?

The vision shifted, showing Hakim the cascade of insights that would flow from these careful observations. In laboratories, scientists traced the branching relationships between species, finding common ancestors in deep time. The tree of life revealed itself not as a metaphor but as a historical fact—all current forms connected through chains of descent and modification stretching back to the first self-replicating molecules.

"We are not fallen angels," a lecturer explained to a shocked audience, "but risen apes. Our nobility comes not from divine decree but from the struggle of countless generations climbing from simplicity toward complexity. Each of us carries in our cells the memory of the primordial ocean. Our very thoughts are shaped by brains evolved for survival on ancient savannas."

Some in the audience were horrified, others exhilarated. One young woman raised her hand: "But if consciousness is merely an adaptation, a survival tool like claws or camouflage, then our deepest experiences—love, beauty, the sense of meaning itself—are they just evolutionary tricks?"

The lecturer paused, clearly struggling with the implications of his own worldview. "Perhaps," he admitted. "Or perhaps consciousness, once emerged, transcends its origins. A cathedral may be built of stones, but it's more than a pile of rocks. So too the mind—evolved from matter but possibly exceeding it."

Hakim watched as the evolutionary revolution rippled outward, transforming every field it touched. Psychology began studying humans as animals with unusually complex behaviours. Sociology examined societies as organisms competing for resources. Even religion was subjected to evolutionary analysis—gods as projections of alpha males, rituals as group bonding mechanisms and afterlife beliefs as denial of mortality's terror.

Yet something strange happened as materialism reached its apparent triumph. The more scientists studied the mechanisms of evolution, the more miraculous the whole process appeared. How did dead molecules organize themselves into self-replicating patterns? How did mere chemistry give rise to the poetry of DNA, storing information across billions of years? How did neural networks generate the unified field of consciousness from their distributed processes?

Hakim found himself in a modern laboratory where these questions pressed with fresh urgency. The scene had jumped forward a century and a half from the naturalist's beach. Now scientists peered not through simple microscopes but through instruments that could visualize individual molecules, trace the firing of single neurons and map the quantum processes in living cells.

"Look at this," a researcher said, displaying a real-time scan of a living brain. "When the subject thinks about moving their hand, we can see the neural preparation beginning several seconds before they report being aware of the intention. Consciousness doesn't initiate action—it ratifies decisions already made by unconscious processes. Free will is an illusion."

But her colleague objected: "You're assuming consciousness equals reportable awareness. What if the neural preparation IS consciousness in action, just below the threshold of reflective self-awareness? What if consciousness operates at many levels, not just the one accessible to verbal report?"

The debate revealed the crisis at materialism's heart. Every attempt to explain consciousness mechanistically ended up assuming consciousness in the explanation. To study the brain required conscious observation. To theorize about evolution required the very intelligence that evolution supposedly explained. The explainer could never be fully explained by its own explanations—it was like trying to see one's own eyes directly.

The vision accelerated through the twentieth century's revelations. Quantum mechanics shattering the clockwork universe, revealing reality as fundamentally probabilistic, observer-dependent. Relativity showing space and time as flexible, perspectival. Chaos theory finding complex order emerging from simple rules. Information theory suggesting reality might be computational rather than material at its base.

Each discovery pointed toward the same conclusion: consciousness wasn't an anomaly in an otherwise mechanical universe. It was revealing itself as fundamental, woven into reality's fabric at every level. The universe wasn't just blindly computing—it was observing itself, collapsing possibility into actuality through the act of measurement that consciousness made possible.

Hakim stood in a cutting-edge physics laboratory where researchers grappled with the measurement problem. "When we're not looking," one explained, "particles exist in superposition—all possible states simultaneously. Only when observed do they 'choose' a definite state. But what counts as observation? A human mind? Any recording device? Any interaction with a larger system?" "The equations work perfectly," another added, "but they don't tell us what's happening in reality. They describe our observations, not what exists between observations. It's as if the universe maintains itself in pure potential until consciousness asks a specific question."

The implications were staggering. Far from being a late addition to a mechanical cosmos, consciousness appeared to be the condition for the cosmos itself. Not creating reality in some crude idealist sense, but participating in its fundamental processes. Observer and observed, mind and matter, inside and outside—all the dualities that had been crystallized were revealing themselves as aspects of a deeper unity that included both without being reducible to either.

As afternoon deepened toward evening, Hakim's journey through modern revelations culminated in a vision of the present moment—laboratories around the world where consciousness studied itself with unprecedented sophistication. Brain scans revealing the neural correlates of every mental state. Artificial intelligence systems exhibiting behaviours indistinguishable from understanding. Quantum computers exploiting the universe's fundamental information-processing capabilities.

Yet for all this technical mastery, the essential mystery remained untouched. *What is it like to be?* How does matter organized in particular patterns generate—or express, or participate in—the felt experience of being someone? The *hard problem of consciousness* loomed larger than ever, not because science had failed but because its very success had clarified what it couldn't address.

A young neuroscientist sat alone in her laboratory after hours, surrounded by millions of dollars of equipment, contemplating the same questions that had haunted humanity since consciousness first recognized itself. "We've mapped every neuron," she said to the empty room. "We've traced every connection. We can predict with 95% accuracy what someone will think before they think it. But we still can't say why there's something it's like to think. We've explained everything except *experience* itself."

She turned off the lights and sat in darkness, feeling her own awareness—not as brain states or neural patterns but as the immediate fact of being present. In that darkness, all the centuries of investigation collapsed into the simple wonder of existing, of *being aware of being aware.*

The vision faded, returning Hakim to his cabin, where

late afternoon sun painted everything golden. He sat quietly, integrating what he'd seen. The journey from the naturalist's idea through quantum uncertainty to the current impasse had shown consciousness backed into a corner—but perhaps it was the corner it had always occupied, the irreducible fact from which everything else proceeded.

Science hadn't failed to explain consciousness—it had succeeded in showing why consciousness couldn't be explained in purely objective terms. Every objective description presupposed the subjective describer. Every map assumed a map-reader. Every theory required a theorist. Consciousness wasn't a problem to be solved, but the *condition that made problem-solving possible.*

Outside his window, the sun continued its descent, and Hakim knew his journey was approaching its culmination. He had seen consciousness know itself through participation in myth, separate itself in civilization and early religion, seek unity through sacred philosophy, exile itself in mechanism, and rediscover itself in matter's mirror. Now would come the final recognition—not a new revelation but the original recognition that had been present all along, waiting patiently for thought to exhaust itself in seeking what was never absent.

The sun that rose knowing he would never see it rise again drew closer to the horizon, and with it, the moment when all seeking would cease in simple recognition of what had always been present, patiently waiting for consciousness to stop looking elsewhere and recognize its own face in the mirror of existence.

# LATE AFTERNOON

## CONSCIOUSNESS CONFRONTS ITS SHADOWS

As the sun descended toward the treeline, painting the sky in shades of rose and gold that belonged to no earthly palette, Hakim felt a different kind of stirring. This was not the pull toward another vision but a gathering of all he had witnessed, a convergence of the morning's journey into a present reckoning. The voices, when they came, arose not from outside but from within—crystallizations of his own understanding into distinct perspectives that demanded to be heard.

He remained in his cabin, but the quality of the space had changed. The room seemed larger, as if it contained not just furniture and books but entire worldviews circling each other like wary dancers. Three presences made themselves known—not as visible forms but as modes of questioning, each carrying the accumulated weight of traditions he had spent his life navigating.

The first voice spoke with the precision of empirical authority—Hakim understood this was his own scientific training personified, given voice and urgency.

"Let's examine the evidence, Hakim," the voice began, cool and measured. "Every mystical experience you've had today can be induced in the laboratory. Temporal lobe stimulation produces the sense of cosmic unity. Ketamine generates out-of-body experiences. Psilocybin reliably triggers the dissolution of self-boundaries you've been experiencing. We've mapped these states down to specific receptor sites and neural pathways."

The voice continued with relentless logic: "You know the literature. Persinger's God helmet creating felt presences through magnetic fields. The replication of near-death experiences through hypoxia. The correlation between mystical experiences and temporal lobe epilepsy. How can you claim consciousness is fundamental when a few milligrams of the right chemical can radically alter it? When brain damage can erase it entirely? When anesthetics can switch it off like a light?"

Hakim felt the weight of these challenges. He had read every study the voice cited. "You're right about the correlations," he responded. "But correlation isn't causation. When I tune a radio to different stations, the circuitry changes with each frequency. Does that mean the radio creates the waves it receives? The brain's changes during altered states might be consciousness focusing itself, not generating itself from nothing."

"Ah, the transmission theory," the scientific voice replied with a hint of condescension. "Attractive but unfalsifiable. Where's your evidence for consciousness existing independently of brains? Show me awareness without neural substrates. Demonstrate memory without hippocampal storage. Present perception without sensory organs. You can't, because consciousness emerges from complex information integration in biological systems.

Period."

Before Hakim could respond, a second voice intervened— his philosophical training given form, carrying centuries of rigorous analysis.

"The empiricist makes a category error," this voice declared. "He assumes consciousness can be studied as an object among objects, forgetting that all objects appear within consciousness. This is the fundamental reflexivity problem—you cannot step outside awareness to study awareness objectively. Every brain scan, every experimental result, every scientific observation occurs within consciousness. How can the contained explain the container?"

The philosophical voice warmed to its theme: "But your position, Hakim, suffers from equal problems. You've had profound experiences today, granted. But what justifies the leap from 'I experienced cosmic consciousness' to 'consciousness is cosmic'? This is the phenomenological fallacy—mistaking the structure of experience for the structure of reality. Perhaps these states reveal only the mind's capacity for self-induced delusion."

"Moreover," the voice continued with surgical precision, "your non-dualism is internally inconsistent. If all is one consciousness, why the appearance of separation? Why the elaborate evolution through time if everything is eternally present? You're multiplying mysteries, not solving them. At least materialism requires only one miracle—the emergence of mind from matter.

You require countless miracles—why consciousness limits itself, why it creates suffering, why it forgets its nature."

Hakim recognized the force of these arguments. He had wrestled with them through sleepless nights and library afternoons. "Perhaps consistency itself is a limited tool," he offered. "Logic works wonderfully within defined domains but breaks down at the extremes. Can logic explain why there's something rather than nothing? Can consistency capture the paradox of self-reference? Reality might be trans-logical, including logic but exceeding it."

"Mystical hand-waving," the philosophical voice dismissed. "The moment you abandon logic, you abandon the possibility of shared understanding. You retreat into private experience, indistinguishable from delusion. How convenient that your position places itself beyond rational critique."

Now the third voice emerged, carrying a different kind of authority—his religious heritage speaking through decades of theological study.

"Both of you miss the essential point," this voice intoned with quiet intensity. "The question isn't whether consciousness can be explained by science or philosophy, but whether human consciousness can encompass the Divine. Hakim, your experiences today—powerful as they've been—skirt dangerously close to the ultimate blasphemy: equating the created with the Creator." The theological voice drew upon scripture and tradition: "Yes,

God is closer than your jugular vein. Yes, the mystics speak of the annihilation of the ego in the Divine presence. But they always maintain the essential distinction—the drop may merge with the ocean, but it doesn't become the ocean. You are created, finite, contingent. To claim identity with the Absolute is the very definition of associating with God."

"I'm not claiming identity," Hakim protested. "I'm recognizing participation. The wave isn't the ocean, but it's not other than the ocean either. The traditional formulation— 'He is not His creation, but His creation is not outside Him'—points to a mystery that transcends simple dualism." "Mystery, yes," the religious voice agreed, "but a mystery with boundaries. The via negativa tells us what God is not, preventing idolatry. The moment you say consciousness itself is divine, you've made an idol of your own awareness. This is the perennial temptation—to mistake the highest human experience for the Divine itself. It's spiritual pride dressed in philosophical garments."

The three voices began to overlap, creating a symphony of challenge:

"Where's your empirical evidence?" "Where's your logical coherence?" "Where's your theological humility?"

Hakim sat with the cacophony, feeling the weight of each tradition's truth. The scientist was right—consciousness correlated with brain states in ways that couldn't be ignored. The philosopher was right—his position did multiply mysteries without clear resolution. The theologian was right—the temptation to inflate human experience to cosmic proportions was real and dangerous.

Yet as he sat with these challenges, something shifted. The voices were all his own, products of consciousness examining itself. The very fact that he could internalize these perspectives, hold them simultaneously, see truth in each while recognizing their limitations—what was this capacity? It wasn't captured by any of the voices individually.

"You're all correct," he said finally. "And all partial. Science maps consciousness's contents brilliantly but can't account for the mapping itself. Philosophy analyzes concepts precisely but can't touch the pre-conceptual awareness in which concepts arise. Theology preserves necessary humility but can't explain why the Absolute would create something absolutely other than itself."

He continued, feeling his way toward integration: "What if consciousness is neither reducible to brains nor simply identical with the Absolute? What if it's the relational field where finite and infinite meet? Not substance but interface, not thing but process, not noun but verb?"

The scientific voice objected: "Word games. Define your terms operationally or admit you're doing poetry, not investigation."

The philosophical voice added: "Relational to what?

You're still assuming consciousness as the field in which relations occur. The circularity remains."

The theological voice warned: "Interface implies two separate domains meeting. You're back to dualism, just with fancier language."

Hakim smiled despite the criticism. "Yes, language fails. It *must* fail. We're trying to speak about that which enables speech. We're trying to think about that which enables thought. Every formulation will be partial because formulation itself is partial. But the failure is instructive—it points beyond itself."

He rose and walked to the window where the late afternoon sun painted the lake in colors  that existed nowhere in the spectrum, yet were undeniably real. "Look," he said to his invisible interlocutors. "The sun's light on water. Is the gold color in the sun? In the water? In my eyes? In my brain? Or is it in the relationship between all of these, arising only in their meeting?"

"False analogy," the scientific voice insisted. "We can trace the exact pathway from photon to perception."

"Missing the point," the philosophical voice corrected. "He's highlighting the emergent nature of qualities."

"Irrelevant," the theological voice concluded. "Natural beauty reflects divine beauty but isn't identical with it."

The voices continued their debate, but Hakim noticed something: they were becoming less distinct, their boundaries blurring. The scientist was making philosophical arguments. The philosopher was citing empirical studies. The theologian was using logical analysis. The divisions that had seemed absolute were revealing themselves as perspectives within a larger conversation.

"This is what I've been trying to say," Hakim realized aloud. "Consciousness isn't any single perspective but the space in which all perspectives arise. It's not scientific or philosophical or theological—it includes all these modes while transcending each. The unity isn't at the level of content but at the level of context."

The voices grew quiet, not silenced but integrated. Hakim felt them settling—not as antagonists but as complementary lenses, each revealing aspects of a truth too large for any single viewpoint to encompass.

Outside, the sun touched the treeline, and the sky began its evening transformation. But for now, Hakim rested in the productive tension of multiple truths, feeling consciousness know itself through the very debates about its nature.

The ghost in the machine, the transcendental subject, the divine spark—all names for the unnameable, all fingers pointing at the moon of awareness itself. And like the moon, consciousness remained serenely itself regardless of the fingers pointing, the names naming, the theories theorizing. The three voices had done their work. They had shown that every attempt to capture consciousness in concepts failed—not because consciousness was absent but because it was too present, too immediate, too obvious to be grasped by the very faculties it enabled.

The eye could not see itself, but it was not, therefore blind.

The sun continued its descent, and Hakim prepared for the final act of the day's drama. All the philosophy, all the science, all the theology had been preparation for this: the simple recognition of what had always been present, waiting patiently for thought to exhaust itself in seeking what was never missing.

# SUNSET

## BECOMING WHOLE

The sun hung low on the horizon, a sphere of molten gold preparing for its daily death and transfiguration. The lake had become a mirror of fire, each small wave a tongue of flame speaking in languages older than words. The very air seemed to thicken with significance, as if the universe were holding its breath before some cosmic revelation.

Hakim walked slowly to the shore, his body heavy with the weight of the day's visions, his mind paradoxically empty and full. The voices had quieted, their arguments dissolved not in resolution but in a kind of exhausted peace.

He had journeyed through humanity's arc of self-knowing, from the cave painters' participation mystique to the modern mind's reflexive puzzlement. And now, as shadows lengthened and the world prepared for night, he stood where he had begun—but everything was different. Or rather, he was different.

He found his familiar granite boulder, still warm from the day's sun, and settled onto it with the careful movements of age and reverence. The stone received him as it always had, indifferent and intimate, solid and yielding. He placed his palms flat against its surface, feeling the minute crystalline structure, the eons of pressure that had formed it, the patience of geological time that made human seeking seem like the briefest flicker.

The sun touched the horizon, and time seemed to slow, each moment expanding to contain infinities. Hakim's awareness, sharpened by the day's journey, noticed everything: the smell of pine resin and lake water, the sound of small waves lapping stone, the feel of cool air on his skin, the play of light transforming the ordinary world into something almost unbearably beautiful.

And then, without warning or fanfare, it happened. Not a vision this time, not a dissolution into other times and places, but something far simpler and more radical.

*The seeking stopped.*

Not through effort or decision, but through a kind of exhaustion so complete it circled back to perfect ease. Like a wave that had travelled across vast oceans, finally reaching shore and releasing its energy in one last surge before settling into stillness.

*"I"* stopped.

Not Hakim—he remained, breathing, feeling, aware. But the "I" that had been seeking, questioning, journeying—that simply ceased.

And in its absence, something else became apparent. Had always been apparent, but hidden by the very search for it.

*Awareness itself.*

Not his awareness, not human awareness, not even living awareness. Simply awareness— the field in which all experience arose and passed away.

It had no qualities because it was the space in which qualities appeared.

It had no location because it was the context for all locations. It had no duration because it contained all time.

Hakim laughed—a quiet sound that seemed to come from the earth itself rather than his throat.

How absurd, the whole journey. Consciousness seeking consciousness was like water seeking wetness.

*The seeker had been the sought.*
*The question had been the answer.*
*The journey out had always been the journey in.*

The sun slipped lower, its bottom edge now kissing the horizon. The sky blazed with colours that existed only in this moment, this unrepeatable configuration of light and atmosphere and perceiving.

Beautiful, yes, but the beauty wasn't separate from the awareness of it. They arose together, depended on each other, and were perhaps different names for the same nameless process.

The scientific voice in him noted that this state correlated with particular brainwave patterns, with decreased activity in the default mode network, with increased gamma wave coherence. All true, all measurable. But like measuring the weight of a poem to understand its meaning. The correlates were real but pointed beyond themselves.

The philosophical voice observed the logical peculiarity of awareness being aware of itself, the strange loop of self-reference that generated a paradox. Also true, also partial. Logic could trace the structure but not taste the actuality.

The theological voice whispered of divine presence, of the *mysterium tremendum*, of the God closer than breath. True again, but incomplete. This was about the sacred as the most intimate fact of existence.

As the sun continued its descent, now half-consumed by the horizon, memories arose unbidden. Not the visions of the morning but personal memories, the texture of a life lived.

He remembered holding his daughters for the first time, feeling a love so intense it seemed to crack open his chest and reorganize everything inside. Where had that love come from? Not from evolutionary imperatives or neurochemical cascades, though these played their roles. It had welled up from some deeper source, as if the universe were loving itself through his temporarily configured form.

He remembered his mother's death and the devastating grief. How her absence had been a presence, how losing her had taught him about the deathless nature of love itself. The form passes, but what moved through the form—did that die? Could awareness itself die? Or did it simply withdraw from one configuration to express through others?

These memories arose and passed like clouds across the sky of awareness, each one poignant, each one partial, each one a note in a symphony too vast for any human ear to hear completely. And beneath them all, supporting them like silence supports sound, was the simple fact of being aware, of consciousness knowing itself through the bittersweet beauty of finite experience.

The sun was three-quarters gone now, the sky beginning its transformation from gold to purple. A few early stars appeared, and Hakim smiled at the poetry of it—ancient light reaching his eyes across impossible distances, the past, touching the present in an eternal now. Those stars might already be dead, their light outlasting them. Or they might blaze on for billions of years after his consciousness had released this particular form. Either way, in this moment, star and awareness met in the simple miracle of seeing.

The sun kissed the horizon with its last sliver of fire. In moments, it would disappear, though Hakim knew this was an illusion—the sun remained constant while the earth turned its face away. How perfect a metaphor for consciousness itself, seeming to arise and set, to be born and die, while remaining eternally present, simply hidden by the turning of attention.

As the final rays painted the sky in impossible purples and roses, Hakim felt his boundaries becoming increasingly theoretical. Where did his body end and the air begin? They exchanged molecules with every breath. Where did his awareness stop and the world start? The seeing and the seen arose together, defined each other, and had no existence apart from their relationship.

This wasn't dissolution in any disordered sense. He remained Hakim, seated on granite, watching the sunset over the lake.

But he was also the watching itself, the space in which Hakim and granite and sunset appeared. Both true simultaneously, like wave and ocean, note and symphony, word and silence.

The sun slipped below the horizon, and for a moment the entire sky blazed with afterglow, as if the day were gathering itself for one last statement before yielding to night. And in that moment, Hakim understood the message that had begun his journey.

"This is the last sunrise" hadn't meant his death, though death would come—to this body, to this configuration of consciousness calling itself Hakim.

It had meant the death of seeking, the end of the search for what had never been absent. Every sunrise after this would be the first, seen with eyes that no longer looked for consciousness elsewhere but recognized it as the looking itself.

He sat in the gathering darkness, feeling no need to return to his cabin. The stars emerged in their ancient patterns, and he recognized them too as consciousness—not conscious beings but patternings of the same awareness that recognized them. The universe seeing itself, knowing itself, celebrating itself through every possible form and formlessness.

Time passed, minutes or hours, he couldn't tell and didn't care. Linear time was just one way consciousness organized its experience. In another sense, this moment contained all moments, was all moments, each now an aperture through which eternity peered into temporality.

Finally, moved not by decision but by the same mysterious promptings that guide birds in migration, Hakim rose from the boulder. He walked slowly back to his cabin, each step a small teaching in presence.

Inside the cabin, he moved with unusual deliberation, as if performing a ritual whose meaning had only now become clear. He lit a single candle, watching the flame spring to life—combustion and consciousness meeting in the simple mystery of light. The room filled with soft shadows that danced and flickered, making the space seem both ancient and newly born.

He sat at his desk where the manuscript lay—pages accumulated over months of writing, his attempt to translate the untranslatable. He picked up his fountain pen and wrote a final entry, his hand steady despite the magnitude of what moved through him:

> "Consciousness never dies because it was never born. What I sought in cells and stars, in philosophy and faith, was always here, closer than breath, simpler than simplicity itself.
>
> We are not beings having an experience of consciousness. We are consciousness having an experience of being.
>
> To whoever finds these words: look for yourself. Not in books or teachings, though these may help, but in the immediate fact of your own awareness. You are what you seek. The journey ends where it began—in the simple recognition of what you have always been.
>
> The sun sets on one horizon only to rise on another. What seems like an ending is a transformation. What appears as death is consciousness releasing one form to express through countless others. Do not mourn the wave returning to the ocean. It was never separate. Remember the sun. It never forgets."

# ABOUT THE AUTHOR

Hakim Ibn Adam writes under a pen name (ḥakīm: sage, physician; Ibn Adam: son of Adam, everyman) that honors both a philosophical tradition and a personal geography—from the Near East to the West, from cell biology to mystical inquiry, from scientific materialism to contemplative philosophy.

For more than thirty years, he studied how cells decide to live or die. But the mechanism could not explain meaning, and the questions accumulated until they demanded a different form of investigation.

His philosophical work asks what it means to be consciousness examining consciousness, what knowledge costs, and whether understanding compensates for permanent displacement.

The exile who studied matter discovered mind. The scientist became a philosopher by necessity.

9 781069 898319